TALL TARGET

"If you have an urge to go out, to take a walk or a ride, take me along as a bodyguard," Canyon O'Grady urged.

The tall man smiled down on O'Grady, who felt short in this man's presence. "I just might do that. Bet you can use that revolver. I used to do a bit of shooting myself, going hunting with a muzzle-loader rifle."

They shook hands and O'Grady felt a tingle go up his arm. This tall man had an aura, a power, a confidence that seemed to be catching. He hoped that the political career of this raw-boned man of the people didn't end here with an assassin's bullet.

Dammit, come hell or high water, no matter how many bullets or how much bloodshed it took, Canyon O'Grady was going to keep Abraham Lincoln alive.

THE
LINCOLN
ASSIGNMENT

by

Jon Sharpe

Ⓢ

A SIGNET BOOK

NEW AMERICAN LIBRARY

A DIVISION OF PENGUIN BOOKS USA INC.

NAL BOOKS ARE AVAILABLE AT QUANTITY DISCOUNTS WHEN USED
TO PROMOTE PRODUCTS OR SERVICES. FOR INFORMATION PLEASE
WRITE TO PREMIUM MARKETING DIVISION, NEW AMERICAN LI-
BRARY, 1633 BROADWAY, NEW YORK, NEW YORK 10019.

Special thanks to Chet Cunningham for his contribution
to this book.

The first chapter of this book previously appeared in *Shadow
Guns*, the fourth volume of this series.

SIGNET TRADEMARK REG. U.S. PAT. OFF. AND FOREIGN COUNTRIES
REGISTERED TRADEMARK—MARCA REGISTRADA
HECHO EN DRESDEN, TN, U.S.A.

SIGNET, SIGNET CLASSIC, MENTOR, ONYX, PLUME,
MERIDIAN AND NAL BOOKS ARE PUBLISHED BY NEW AMERI-
CAN LIBRARY, A DIVISION OF PENGUIN BOOKS USA INC., 1633
BROADWAY, NEW YORK, NEW YORK 10019

FIRST PRINTING, JANUARY, 1990

1 2 3 4 5 6 7 8 9

PRINTED IN THE UNITED STATES OF AMERICA

Canyon O'Grady

His was a heritage of blackguards and poets, fighters and lovers, men who could draw a pistol and bed a lass with the same ease.

Freedom was a cry seared into Canyon O'Grady, justice a banner of the heart.

With the great wave of those who fled to America, the new land of hope and heartbreak, solace and savagery, he came to ride the untamed wildness of the Old West.

With a smile or a six-gun, Canyon O'Grady became a name feared by some and welcomed by others but remembered by all . . .

August 1858, on the Illinois prairie, where the life of a man—and the future of an entire nation—depends on a quick wit and a straight shot . . .

1

Man-sized shadows melted in and out of the three-A.M. darkness around the front and back doors of the small two-story house. Liquid spilled from a can against the front door and door frame, then more splashed on the side of the house. A figure tore stinker matches off a wax plug and lighted the fluid.

Flames quickly rose up the door and ate into the dry wood. At the back of the house the same procedure took place and in minutes both doorways blazed brightly.

In the early-morning hours nearly everyone in Ottawa, Illinois, was sleeping soundly. Only a milkman heading for his barn saw the flames. He rushed up to the house and pounded on the walls and shouted. Then he found a rock and threw it through an upstairs window. He slammed a brick through a downstairs window and at last he heard a voice from inside.

"What in the world is the matter?" a voice brayed from the window upstairs. An angular, whiskered face stared past the broken glass. "What seems to be the problem down there?"

"Nothing, sir, if you wish to become a well-roasted duck. Your house is on fire!"

Three figures in the shadows of the house next door backed deeper into the darkness as another man ran up. Lights began to glow across the street and soon more people rushed to the fire.

The tall man in work pants, unbuttoned shirt, and unlaced shoes vaulted through a downstairs window clutching a small leather briefcase. "I don't understand," he said. "The fire was at the front door *and* the back door. How could that happen?"

A crowd had gathered now, but there was no chance to save any of the furniture or goods inside. The blaze spread so rapidly in the dry wooden structure that not even a bucket brigade was tried.

A large, heavy man ran up, looking around frantically. "Has anyone seen the man who lives here?" he asked someone.

The tall man ambled over to the questioner. "Harvey, just relax, everything is fine. I even saved my briefcase and my speeches and my research."

"I told you it was serious," Harvey said, looking up at the rawboned man who stood six-feet four-inches. "I told you, Mr. Lincoln, that we had to take those threats seriously."

"Now, Harvey, just calm down. I'm fine. Sort of makes me think maybe Douglas is having second thoughts about agreeing to these debates. Somebody is getting nervous, and I enjoy that. Besides, that old black suit was about used up and I could use a new hat. I think I'll get one of those black toppers."

Harvey took Lincoln by the arm and led him over to a carriage. They got in and went to the only hotel in town, where the heavy man rented a room on the third floor in front.

Upstairs, Harvey turned the room's only chair around and put it against the room's only door and sat down. "I don't care if you agree, Mr. Lincoln, but I'm going to sit right here and see that nobody gets into this room the rest of the night. You might as well go back to sleep. You don't have any appointments today until almost noon.''

Abe Lincoln sat on the hotel bed and thought about the fire. Someone had started the blaze at both doors. Were they hoping to trap him inside and burn him to a cinder? Or were they just trying to scare him out of debating with U.S. Senator Stephen A. Douglas? He wasn't sure. But he wasn't going to scare.

He'd been to the House of Representatives from Illinois for one term. He had a passion for politics and now he hoped he could defeat Douglas for his Senate seat in the upcoming election. Win or lose, making this race and having these debates would be to his benefit. His Republican advisers said he had a good chance to whip Douglas. A good performance in the seven debates was of prime importance and the first would be held in Ottawa in two weeks.

Lincoln took off his still-untied shoes and stretched out on the hotel bed. His feet hung off the end by a dozen inches. He was used to that. He drifted off to sleep, reflecting on what his opening statement should be in the first debate.

President James Buchanan leaned back in the big leather chair behind his massive desk and sighed. He was sixty-seven years old and felt the full and massive weight and responsibility of being president smashing down on his narrow shoulders. He'd held the office for two years and it seemed right then like twenty.

He wiped a hand over his face and stared at the man across the desk from him. "Canyon O'Grady, I know you usually take on more exciting jobs than this one, but this could turn out to be of vital importance to our nation. You know we're having an election in two years. Already the candidates are lining up for this job. I'm not running again. I believe in the democratic process. Let the people speak. We are a government by the people and for the people. And I don't like the idea of seeing the deck stacked in anyone's favor, especially the Republicans.''

O'Grady sat on the edge of the chair, his back ramrod-straight, his flame-red hair cut neatly for a change. He was attired in his best black suit and string tie. He didn't have the slightest idea where President Buchanan was going with this line of talk.

"We've been hearing rumors for weeks, and at last we have some idea of what is going on. We fear that there is a plot afoot to limit the ballot for president, perhaps stack it in favor of one or the other of the parties. I won't stand for that.

"We're afraid the target is Senator Stephen A. Douglas, of Illinois. He's one of the leading Democratic candidates. Reports indicate that a team of deadly assassins is after the senator.''

"Do we have any names, descriptions?''

"Yes, we do. I'll turn you over to my assistant, Jamiston Priestly, who will be your contact. He'll give you the details. I just want to be sure you understand how seriously I take this mission. We could be dealing with history here. If we don't catch the assassins and Douglas is killed, this nation would suffer a great loss.''

"Yes, Mr. President, I understand.''

"I hope you do, Mr. O'Grady. I'm not out to protect only Senator Douglas even if he is from my party. This other fellow, his opponent Lincoln, is said to be coming up fast as a Republican candidate for the nomination. Of course, I want you to put an end to this threat by jailing or eliminating the terrorizers. That way we'll be protecting both the possible presidential candidates.''

The president peaked his fingers and stared over them. "Now, Mr. O'Grady, if you have any more questions, I'm sure Mr. Priestly can take care of them."

O'Grady stood. "Thank you, Mr. President."

President Buchanan looked up, fatigue evident in his eyes. O'Grady knew the man was feeling his age now and sagging under the pressures of the job.

"Stop them, O'Grady," Buchanan ordered. "Stop the ruffians!"

A half-hour later, Agent O'Grady got all the details from Jamiston Priestly.

Priestly was a medium-sized man, about average height at five-seven. He dressed with care, and with a little more flair than his lawyer background would indicate. His eyes were large, with lids held back to expose more of the eyeball than usual. He smoked a long black cigar which he pulled on, looked at, relit, or waved with continuously during the meeting. O'Grady guessed the man was never without the burning torch. Priestly motioned to a chair beside his desk.

"Mr. O'Grady, we have definite evidence now that there is a conspiracy afoot to interfere in our internal affairs in the most heinous way. Certain foreign powers, exporters and shipping tycoons, have come together and quite simply hired some American assassins who will kill anyone for enough money.

"Money has been paid, half down, the rest on completion. We think we know the target and the approximate time the attack could take place. Your job is to stop them any way you can, including killing all four. Are those orders unquestionably clear?"

"I have a license to kill them?"

"Precisely. There are four of them, three men and a woman. They are all U.S. citizens, all have records of arrests, convictions, and two have served prison time, another jail time. The woman has not been in

13

jail, but is bound to them strongly. "You've heard of Senator Douglas, I assume."

"Yes."

"We think he's the target. However, our information is not specific. Since both he and Abraham Lincoln will be appearing in a series of debates coming up shortly, both men could be targets. Each might be a presidential candidate in 1860. Do you have any suggestions?"

"Yes, call off the debates, put both men under tight security," O'Grady said.

Priestly smiled. "You don't know much about politics, Mr. O'Grady. That would be like drowning them in a bathtub. A politician exists for public exposure, public speaking, shaking hands, walking his district. He's an outgoing animal, not one to keep locked in a room somewhere with ten armed guards around him. We can't stop or alter the debates. They must go on as planned. Neither man would allow any change."

O'Grady waved away some of the cigar smoke and shook his head. "Mr. Priestly, you're making this harder."

"Not only hard, it may be impossible. If an assassin has a powerful-enough urge to kill someone to the point of sacrificing his own life to do it, then there is no way to stop him. His target can't be protected every minute of every day for the rest of the target's life."

"But we're talking about a week or two. How long will the debates last?"

"I'm not sure, and it may not be a factor. From what we have learned, the attack is to take place before or during the first debate, which is two weeks from today in Ottawa, a small town to the west of Chicago."

"Two weeks away? You just found out about it?"

"Two days ago. It took you two days to get here."

14

He handed O'Grady a sheaf of papers in a folder. "Here is what we know about the people. We have good descriptions and names and some of the ways they used to make a living. Mostly armed robbery: a train once, stores, then banks. Usually they kill one person in the bank to frighten everyone else.

"You can take that with you. I have you on a six-thirty train tonight for Chicago. You'll be there to-morrow about this time, then continue to Ottawa on another train. It's about eighty miles on west."

"Who's behind the plot?"

"We're not sure. Foreign shipping interests, it seems. We think that they are afraid that Senator Douglas will start a civil war, which will ruin the United States as a market for their goods."

"Doesn't seem reasonable," O'Grady said.

"Oh, but it does. Any one shipper sending goods to Charleston, say, or New Orleans, could lose millions and millions of dollars if those ports were blockaded. Same for shipping into New York or Philadelphia if those ports were closed. The monetary motive here is extremely strong and well-founded."

"And we have two weeks before the first debate?"

"Unless you can stop them before that time. You'll have plenty of time to read the reports and biographies on the train. Do you want any help? I could send you two or three good people for assistance."

"Sorry. I work alone. It's easier that way and I don't have to worry about shooting one of my helpers."

"Just an idea. But remember, I take my orders from President Buchanan, just like you do. Now, let's go to the accounting office, make a draw for your expenses, and get you on that train for Chicago."

2

Canyon O'Grady took off his tie and got comfortable in the sleeping-car seat, which would soon be made up into a bed. He pulled out the folder of material from Priestly and looked at the details on the assassins.

On top were drawings of the men and woman and a page or two about each one. He picked up the top one and began to read:

Flint Nymon, twenty-eight years old, native of Georgia. Wanted in that state and eight others for murder, bank robbery, rape, train robbery, and various other robbery charges. Known to have killed six men. Armed at all times and extremely dangerous.

Physical description: five feet eight inches tall, 145 pounds. Lean, thin face, often four or five days' growth of beard. No beard or mustache. Hair kept cut short in businessman's style. Meticulous in dress. Prefers fancy vests and pocket watch with fob.

Polite, some education. Respectful of women and young girls, but kills men without flinching or seemingly a second thought. Can be devious and patient. Is said to have had some acting experience and good with makeup and costumes.

Never underestimate Nymon. He's a marksman, drunk or sober. If found, alert local police or sheriff's office to aid in capturing. Has bragged that he will never be taken alive.

No known scars on exposed body. No limps or disfigurements. Has formed a group called Nymon's Raiders. Expert horseman and woodsman, equally at home in fancy ballroom. Excellent dancer and charmer of women.

May have with him one Marcella Quiney, detailed here.

O'Grady went to the next sheet. It was set up much the same way about another member of the group.

Dade Matzner, twenty-six, five feet four inches tall, weight 120. Nicknamed Shorty. His favorite weapon is a sawed-off shotgun with double barrels. He is slender, with long blondish hair that is unkempt. Wears a full beard and mustache.

Not particular about his clothes. Often wears same items for two weeks at a time and his clothes can become an identifying point. Prefers a low-crowned western black hat with flat brim. Usually wears a pair of six-guns. Can shoot well with both hands.

Not a talker. Seldom says a word during a robbery or holdup. Has no use for women, is not married.

Kills without remorse and often with little thought of the consequences. Seems to get no thrill from killing. Thinks it is just a part of his job as a bank robber.

Has long list of states where he is wanted for murder, robbery, train robbery, and mayhem. Dangerous when cornered.

No record of killing for hire, but some evidence that such may be the case. Always armed and considered highly dangerous and at times irrational.

O'Grady frowned. One dandy who likes the girls and kills without remorse. Another, a short man who doesn't like women and is irrational at times and kills like a machine. Nice group to go with to a Sunday-school picnic. He looked at the next member of the gang.

Crunch Hoke, thirty-four, six feet tall, 230 pounds or more, broad shoulders, powerful man. Can't read or write. May have suffered from a head injury. A lackey for Nymon. Worships him. Would probably die for him if Nymon asked him to. Has the courage and bravery of an idiot, no sense, or fear, of danger and death.

Excellent shot with pistol or rifle. Marksman with Sharps breach-loading .52-caliber percussion rifle. Crunch is said to be able to hit targets from half a mile away with precision.

Got his nickname of Crunch when he caught two men and bashed their heads together, killing both.

Wanted in four states, two for murder by shooting, two for deaths from beatings with his bare hands, and for train robbery.

Tender and thoughtful and respectful with women, perhaps thinking of all women as his mother or his sisters. Has no intimate relations with women.

Armed and extremely dangerous, depending on companions. If found alone, approach with deliberate caution. Do not attempt to capture single-handedly. Call on lawmen for help.

O'Grady settled back in the seat. The light was starting to fade. He opened the blind on the window and spread out the three sheets and looked at them again, then turned to the fourth one.

The drawing here was more interesting. A woman, a pretty woman. He read the flier.

Marcella Quiney, twenty-two, redheaded, five feet three inches tall. Slender, perhaps 100 pounds. Former prostitute from Atlanta. Once a dealer in a gambling hall, so she is good with cards. Little formal education but has read widely in the classics and can quote Shakespeare, Samuel Johnson, and is fond of a new poet, Walt Whitman.

An attractive woman with a good figure who is not

adverse to using her sexual charms to help her current lover, Flint Nymon. Often travels ahead or slightly behind the other three and uses public transportation when possible.

Dresses expensively in gowns and dresses not possible for the average woman to afford. Uses jewelry in high fashion and good taste. (All her jewelry is stolen.)

Is known to carry a derringer in either her reticule or a pocket in her skirts.

No outstanding warrants or wants on this person.

The steward came by to make up Canyon's berth, so he went to the back of the car and stood on the small outside platform, listening to the clack-clack of the train as it rushed through the night.

A few minutes later, he opened the door to the sleeper car and found the aisle between the curtained berths lighted by four kerosene lamps suspended from the top of the car. He returned to his berth and found a young woman vainly trying to get into the one just over his. He watched her a moment and saw a slender ankle peek from under her long robe.

"Miss, could I help you?" O'Grady asked, putting on his most gallant smile.

She turned and the hood to her robe slipped a bit and he saw she had red hair. Her face held a frown, but slowly it ebbed away.

"I just don't see how they expect a lady to get into these things," she said, and the southern accent was not only obvious but the tone generously applied with pride.

Southern, redhead. The words brought up immediate pictures of the description of Marcella Quiney. He squelched the idea at once. "One way to beat the problem is to get a lower berth. I could trade with you."

"No, that won't be necessary."

"You might try stepping on the edge of the lower berth, or we can call the steward for a ladder they have."

"Oh, I never thought of stepping on your berth." She lifted her foot and the movement revealed a stretch of pale white skin almost to her knee. She never hesitated, swinging up and into the top berth with a quick movement. The nicely shaped bare leg vanished.

A moment later her head poked out of the middle of the curtain that hid her bunk. "Thank you ever so much, kind sir. That was gallant of you. Good night." The curtain closed with a snap.

"You're welcome," he said softly, and sat in his berth and closed the curtains.

So, enough on the speculation about the southern beauty sleeping just inches away from him. She undoubtedly was not Marcella Quiney. He thought about the profiles he had read on each of the four. He still had no starting spot. Just the small town where a political debate would take place in two weeks.

Damned little to get started on. Maybe some of the other papers would give him a clue that would get his work moving. He wished this sleeper had gaslights, then he could have read for hours yet.

As it was, he settled down, slid out of half of his clothes, and went to sleep. He'd be up at daylight and finish his reading then.

Chicago was big and noisy and dusty. O'Grady figured there were more than 40,000 people in the place. It hadn't yet realized that it was a city, and it looked like a small town with a city growing up right inside it.

Canyon caught a train heading west after only a three-hour wait and stepped off at Ottawa shortly after seven o'clock that evening. He found a room at the small town's only hotel and checked over his reading material again.

All day he had digested what Priestly had provided him. He had backgrounds on Lincoln and Douglas. It seemed a mismatch when he looked at the election record. Lincoln had been a congressman for only one two-year term from Illinois.

Stephen A. Douglas, on the other hand, had been a U.S. senator from Illinois for six years. He was the overwhelming favorite to be reelected in this race against the one-term congressman. Douglas was also one of the two leading contenders for the Democratic nomination in the 1860 presidential election.

Still, Lincoln was a fighter. He had made fifty speeches for the Republican ticket in the 1856 presidential election. Some said he was a strong contender for the Republican nomination for president in 1860. "Who else have the Republicans got but honest Abe Lincoln?" was one of the jokes in the political chatter around the country.

O'Grady absorbed it all, then went over the agreement for the debates. Douglas at first hadn't wanted to give the younger man a forum to be seen and heard by the people of Illinois. Then it had started to look as if Douglas was afraid of debate but felt he had to go through with it.

His right-hand man and campaign chairman was Randolph P. Alacron, a former congressman who had led Douglas to his senatorial victory. He was the first man O'Grady would talk to. Canyon's second appointment would be with the man doing the similar job for Lincoln, Onan Sanborn.

Both Lincoln and Douglas were said to be hard at work studying the issues of the day, especially the slavery question, which permeated every political discussion on the national level these days. Something was brewing there that could explode at any time. O'Grady used to worry about it, but at last he realized there was nothing he could do to stop the eventual explosion. He just wished he knew how and where it was going to happen.

He enjoyed having two coal-oil lamps to light in the hotel room, and reread most of the papers before he lay down to go to sleep. He had no plan yet, other than trying to get the participants to limit their public appearances and public movements as much as possible before the debates. He had worked out a summary of what the government suspected about the danger, and he decided to tell the campaign managers, then ask for restrictions on the candidates' movement. It was a start.

Then he would alert the La Salle county sheriff and see what kind of a man he was and what kind of help he could expect—if he needed it.

With that agenda in mind, Canyon blew out both lights and settled down. He had locked his door with the skeleton-type key, but left it turned halfway around in the lock. No other key could be inserted without turning his key around and pushing it out, which was nigh impossible to do from the outside. He didn't even push a chair back under the door handle for added security.

No one knew who he was or why he was in town. Tomorrow night it would be different.

The next morning dawned bright and sunny. After breakfast at the hotel's dining room, Canyon went out to reconnoiter the town. As he passed the small county courthouse, he saw the sheriff's office sign. Canyon paused, then shrugged and went up the sidewalk to the door deciding to see the sheriff first while he was here.

He pushed open the door to find that the office was

a bustle of action. Three deputies walked from one door to another talking quietly.

An inside door opened and a man came out wearing a black suit with a sheriff's star on its broad lapel.

"Men, we just have a confirmation from an eyewitness. The bank in La Salle, ten miles down the road, was robbed by a gang who usually work in Missouri and points west. For some reason they came up this far. They could be paying us a visit next.

"You men heard of them, I'm sure. Call themselves Nymon's Raiders. It's them for sure. The big tall one, the short, ugly one, and Nymon himself. The bastard killed one of the bank clerks to 'shut him up.' I'm going down there right now on the morning cattle train and taking two men with me to lend assistance. Rest of you stay here, keep the peace, and be ready."

O'Grady pushed up to the sheriff and held out his identification card that had been sealed in isinglass. "Sheriff, I'm Canyon O'Grady and I need to talk to you. We can talk on our way to La Salle."

3

Sheriff Bayne Tillery of La Salle County was not a man to turn down help. He stood tall and thin with sagging jowls on a rather fleshy face. His lower eyelids drooped giving him a hound-dog look, but the bright-blue orbs snapped with excitement.

The cattle train was not on time, so the sheriff hired a rig at the livery and he drove as Canyon O'Grady explained to him exactly who he was and why he was in Ottawa.

"Good, good, glad you're here. I take all of the help from anywhere I can find it. Heard that there would be some federal people in town for the debate. Didn't expect anyone quite so soon. You say this same Nymon gang might be coming to town to shoot down our debaters?"

"We're certain of it, Sheriff Tillery. At least they're going to try. My job is to stop them."

"They had a big job like that coming up, why they go ahead and rob a bank ten miles away?"

"Nymon thinks he can do anything and get away with it. He probably got restless going for a couple of weeks without killing anyone. He's a monster who has to be stopped."

"Hope the bank people or Chief Jetster over at La Salle can tell us which way they headed. The chief is an old-timer, not much of a modern-day lawman, but

24

in his prime he could outshoot half a dozen big-time outlaws I could name.''

They rode along in silence. There were two deputies in the back seat. For a moment O'Grady wished that the cattle train had been on time. Then it would have taken them only twenty minutes to make the trip on the train. This way they would use up two hours.

During the ride, O'Grady had some time to tell the three lawmen more about Nymon's Raiders and their habits, and about the woman who often traveled near them but not with them. "The short one with his sawed-off shotgun is probably the most dangerous. He killed six people in one bank robbery because one woman wouldn't stop crying and a man yelled insults at him. Don't take any chances with any of them.''

The decision not to wait for the train was the correct one, since the buggy arrived in La Salle city before the cattle train did that morning.

The bank had been robbed the day before, just at closing time. It showed all of the hallmarks of a Nymon robbery: people tied up and put on the floor; front door locked at closing time and the blinds pulled.

Without a passerby hearing the single pistol shot in the bank, the robbery might have gone unnoticed for hours. The gang got out the back door just as a deputy ran into the alley. He was shot down and wounded but not killed. He returned fire and thought he hit one of the three who charged away on horses.

Chief Jetster was at the bank when the delegation arrived. The chief was about sixty, shrunken, shriveled, a pruneish face that had seen too much death and lawbreaking. He squinted at Canyon O'Grady and grinned.

"Always did like my lawmen to be redheaded,'' he said, and gripped O'Grady's hand strongly. "Hope you can help us find the bastards. Last we knew they was headed down toward the river and Starved Rock. Not even sure if they kept together. Looks like they split up at one point.

"I knew you'd be here, Tillery, so I waited on the posse until you came. I don't ride none too good no more, so I'm sending my top man, Willis. I got six boys all ready out front. I brought along three extra saddled horses."

Sheriff Tillery asked one of his deputies to run to the livery and rent a horse and catch up with them.

The posse mounted up and rode.

Off the main road and the railroad tracks, the country was not as heavily populated. As they neared the good-sized Illinois River to the south, they found fewer and fewer small farms and ranches until the country was virtually empty.

Ten of them riding across the open fields made too big a show for the way O'Grady wanted it. But for the moment he was stymied. If they could run this bunch down and eliminate them right here, it would solve his main problem in a rush.

Their tracker, a man named Jingo, stopped a quarter of a mile from the river and waited for the main party.

"Went two ways from here, Captain," Jingo said. "Looks like two horses moving this way and two the other way."

"Where did they get the fourth rider?" Sheriff Tillery asked. "I thought you said only three horses left town."

"That's right, Sheriff. Three horses, but there are definitely two moving each way out here now."

Sheriff Tillery looked at the local deputy. "Your posse, Sheriff," Willis said.

"We split up half the men each way," Sheriff Tillery decided. "Willis, you take half the men. I'll take my men and O'Grady. Find anything important, get off three shots. Move out."

Sheriff Tillery talked like an old cavalry trooper, which he was. They followed the track angling toward the river. Two miles down they found a cold campfire and places where horses had spent several hours. On a piece of paper pegged to the ground with a small stake was a message.

"Sorry, Sheriff, we're gone. We waited for you. Where have you been?"

It was not signed. Before they mounted up, the other half of the posse came riding in.

"Bastard is playing games with us," Sheriff Tillery said.

They rode back on the new trail that O'Grady picked up as he and the tracker made half-circles around the camp. The outlaws were still moving to the east along the river.

Two miles farther upstream they came to a farmhouse. A shotgun boomed toward them while they were a hundred yards away.

"State your business," a man bellowed from the front door of the house.

"Sheriff Tillery and posse. We're looking for some killer bank robbers."

"Oh." A man came out of the house unarmed.

"Sheriff, yeah, come on in. Bastards left not an hour ago heading east. Stayed half the day, ate up most of my grub. You say they killed somebody?"

The sheriff got a quick description of the men.

"Oh, there was this pretty girl along with them. She looked too refined and well-dressed to be with them, but she said she was. They rode east along the river far as I could see."

The sheriff thanked him and moved them out. O'Grady and the tracker took turns leapfrogging each other to make sure the trail went the same way. The posse rode at a canter or a gallop, depending how far away the trackers were. They made good time.

O'Grady had just come through a small arm of a woods thick with willow and some heavy brush when he felt wind whip past him, and a moment later he heard the crack of a rifle. He dived off his mount to the left away from the sound and rolled back into the brush. He lay still for a moment, then lifted his head so he could see through the light screen ahead.

Five hundred yards upstream on a slight rise he saw a figure on a horse. The man sat there a minute, then worked with what must have been his long gun, perhaps reloading it. A minute later the figure rode down the slope and out of sight.

The tracker came riding up. He'd heard the shot. "You hit?"

"No, but tell the sheriff I'm going to try to go around them and cut them off. They know we're here now and have a rear guard. Be careful."

O'Grady kicked his horse in the flanks and rode directly toward the river. Once inside the cover he rode as fast as he could through the light brush and trees. When he had to, he went down to the riverbank, where low water had left a hard-packed avenue.

Twice he poked out to the very edge of the cover and looked on east. He could spot no horsemen. The third time, he waited until he had pushed his horse close to exhaustion with three long gallops. He dropped off and edged out to the thin brush and looked upstream.

Four horsemen rode along less than two hundred yards ahead of him. There were three men and a woman who sat in a fancy side saddle. Although there was a rifle in the boot on the saddle, it wasn't his, and Canyon had no idea how accurate it was or which side of absolute straight it would shoot. So, it would be best to get ahead of them and drive them back toward the posse.

O'Grady squirmed deeper into the brush and got to his horse, then rode along the riverbank behind the cover at a lope. After what he figured was a quarter of a mile, he pulled out the rifle from the boot and looked at it. He wasn't even sure what make it was, but saw it was loaded with one shot. He looked at it again and saw it was a 1855 Springfield, a .58-caliber weapon.

Canyon worked his way through the brush on foot until he came to the meadow just beyond the river woods. The four riders now came toward him at an efficient pace but in no great run for their lives.

He should wait until they came within thirty yards of him and pick out Flint Nymon and blow him straight into hell, where he was long overdue. But he couldn't. He'd give them a chance to surrender. He cocked the heavy rifle and waited. At this range a slight deviation in aim would mean little, but if he were firing it from a thousand yards, it would make a big difference in the impact area.

The four riders came forward. From time to time the largest man on the white horse rode to the rear for a look at the backtrail, then came and joined the others. They were talking and laughing about something as they came toward him.

When they were about thirty yards away from where he lay in the brush, O'Grady bellowed at them, "Government agents. Raise your hands and surrender!"

At the first word the four spurred and jerked their mounts around in four different directions. One rider came almost straight at Canyon. It was the man with the shotgun, which he swung up and fired.

O'Grady tracked him a moment, then fired, and the heavy slug caught the rider in the upper right arm and

29

nearly tore the limb from his body. It jolted him out of the saddle and dumped him on the ground, where he brayed in terrible pain and fury.

None of the others looked back. There was no time for more than one shot, and he had no means to follow them. He drew his pistol and fired twice at the fleeing bank robbers, but they continued to fly down the way they had been going, but now they vanished into the brush some fifty yards ahead.

O'Grady held his pistol ready as he rushed out to the wounded man. He came up on him slowly, made sure he could see both the man's hands and that neither held a weapon.

"Easy, Matzner," O'Grady said as he walked up. "Don't do anything stupid and get yourself killed. With your record and all the wanteds on you, I should just blow your head off right now."

Dade Matzner looked up in white-hot anger. His whole body shook with pain and he stared down at the revolver on his right hip, where it was now spotted with his own blood.

"If I could get to it, I'd kill you, whoever you are."

"Your killing days are over. Your sawed-off shotgun didn't help you any this time. You have your share of the bank loot in your saddlebags?"

"Why? You want me to buy you off? I give you a thousand dollars and you get me to a doctor? How does that sound, U.S. Government Agent?"

"Sounds fine, except the only doctor you'll see will be when he visits you in a jail cell."

O'Grady could see one of Tillery's deputies spurring his horse forward, his rifle in one hand as he raced up toward the sound of the weapons firing.

The other posse members galloped closely behind him.

They dismounted and relieved the gunman of his

sidearm, then one of the men took bandages from his saddlebags and stopped the flow of blood from the killer's arm.

"Well, you got one of them. That only leaves three," Sheriff Tillery said.

"Where are Nymon and the others heading?" O'Grady asked the outlaw.

"Straight to hell, same as you," Matzner said. One of the deputies backhanded Matzner and he looked up and snorted. "That the best you can do, Rover Boy? I've had a dozen women who hit harder than that."

Another deputy came back with Matzner's horse and O'Grady went through the saddlebags. He found nearly two thousand dollars in paper money and gold coins. In the other side was an envelope with two sheets of paper.

O'Grady unfolded them and looked them over quickly. They were descriptions of A. Lincoln and S. Douglas, the date of the first debate and the location.

The notes on the second page were the most interesting.

Enclosed please find five hundred dollars to use for expenses and in partial as an advance. The remaining ten thousand dollars will be ready for you at the Willoughby Inn in Ottawa, the evening after both parties have gone to their heavenly reward. We wish you good fortune and straight shooting in this endeavor, which we trust will be mutually beneficial.

There was no signature. Not even an initial.

O'Grady passed the papers to Sheriff Tillery. When the lawman had read the paper, O'Grady held out his hand. "You have all you need on Dade Matzner here on bank robbery and murder, even if he didn't pull the trigger. I need the paper for my hunt for the other three and their generous employer."

"Yes, that's true."

"Sheriff, I'd like this whole thing kept just between you and me. None of your people need to know about it yet. Those who do, tell them it's strictly confidential. If it gets to the point that the debate is about to take place, you may have to call it off to prevent a riot. That's an acceptable procedure.

"Now, I think it's time we get Matzner here back to La Salle and into jail. I'd suggest you put out a point man and a backtrail guard and an outrider on each side. We don't want anything to happen to him before he can be properly hung. Nymon is the kind of man who might try to take Matzner away from us before we get back to town."

4

Nymon's Raiders didn't try to rescue their captured man as the posse rode back to La Salle. Chief Jetster was delighted with the arrest and hustled Matzner into jail and called a doctor to bandage up Matzner's shoulder.

"Gonna get a trial set for next week," Jetster said. "Want the people of La Salle to know that we caught one of the killers and got part of the money back." The banker was on hand to claim part of his missing cash.

The afternoon train back to Ottawa would be coming through in an hour. O'Grady and the sheriff waited for it and sent the two deputies back with the buggy.

Two hours later, O'Grady continued his interrupted walk through the town. He decided to talk to Onan Sanborn first. He knocked on the door of a small white house just off the main street and was greeted by a short, fat man who had the face of a fox: sharp, a long nose, beady eyes, and thinning reddish hair.

"Yes?"

"Mr. Sanborn?"

"That's right."

"My name is Canyon O'Grady. I'm from Washington, D.C., and I need to talk to you for a few minutes about the upcoming debate between Mr. Lincoln and Senator Douglas."

"That's my job," Sanborn said. He waved O'Grady into the living room of the small house. It was sparsely furnished, and everything looked as if it were there on a temporary basis.

"I'm a United States government agent working with the Justice Department, Mr. Sanborn," O'Grady said. He took out the isinglass-covered card with the authorization direct from President Buchanan on it, and showed it to the man.

"I see. That's quite impressive. But how does our little debate have any bearing on the federal government?"

"It could have a great bearing, Mr. Sanborn. The Justice Department has received information that there is a plot to assassinate one or both of the participants in the debate."

"Assassina—" The idea hit Sanborn hard and he frowned and took a step backward. "Perhaps we should sit down, Mr. O'Grady. You're serious about this?"

They sat on chairs facing each other and O'Grady went over the facts as he knew them. He told Sanborn about the capture of one of Nymon's Raiders and the incriminating letter the man had had with him.

"You think Senator Douglas is this frightened of Mr. Lincoln that he's arranged to have him shot?"

"Not really. Justice thinks that Senator Douglas is the real target. Some people are afraid that his slavery stance will bring war that will ruin a fine shipping trade. And back in Washington they don't know that *both* Douglas and Lincoln are targets."

"Good Lord! A prudent man would call off the debates at once."

O'Grady laughed. "True, but these are not prudent men; these are politicians. I'm told that would be impossible. Even if we did, the men would still be targets. Better to let the debate plans go forward now so we can try to nab the rest of the gang before they know we're onto them."

"Yes, yes," Sanborn said, nodding. "We both agree on that. Something that happened last night you may not know about. Mr. Lincoln's house burned to the ground. It was a rented place, and he was there alone. Both the front and back doors were doused with kerosene and set afire. Do you think that could have been connected with the plot by these men?"

O'Grady wrinkled his brow in surprise and then thought about it a moment. "It could have been part of the overall plot. But I'd guess it wasn't. The Nymon gang would rather use a gun and be sure of the results. Perhaps it was an accident?"

"Not both doors at once, and not with the distinct odor of kerosene on the burned door frames. Someone may have been only trying to scare him. This sort of thing has happened to Mr. Lincoln before. He has strong beliefs, you know, and isn't afraid to speak his mind."

Sanborn wiped his freely perspiring forehead. "Do we tell the candidates about this new and serious threat?"

"That's up to you, Mr. Sanborn, but I'd recommend that we don't. We want everything to look normal. If the candidates know about it, they might say something or do something the conspirators would notice. We don't want to scare off the outlaws."

Sanborn stood, clasped his hands behind his back, and paced the length of the room three times. When he looked up, he nodded. "Yes, I agree. Where are you staying, at the hotel?"

"Yes."

"I want to be able to get in contact with you at any time. I'll hire some more security—"

"No, Mr. Sanborn. That, also, could scare off the killers."

"But if they strike tomorrow, what defense will we have?"

"I have the notion that they will wait until the day of the debate. There will be lots of people in town, lots of strangers. The killers would have an easier chance to get away."

"Yes, I see your point. That's good reasoning. All right. We'll be on our guard. I'm certainly going to start carrying a revolver—a small one and out of sight—but I'll have one. If there's anything you want us to do, just send me a note or stop by here and see me. I'll have a young man here to answer the door after today, so we can stay in touch."

O'Grady thanked him and walked out to the street. A short time later he walked up to the door of another house on the other side of town and talked to Randolph P. Alacron. He was a tall, thin, sparse man with the dignified air of a judge. No one called him Randy. O'Grady got almost the same reaction from Alacron. In the end he got a vow of secrecy from Alacron about the threat, and a promise to cooperate with O'Grady and to keep in close touch.

Back on the street, O'Grady felt his stomach rumbling and looked at his pocket watch: it was near four-thirty. That's when he realized he hadn't had any lunch. He walked back to the hotel and asked the clerk if there were any messages.

"No, sir, Mr. O'Grady. However, there is someone waiting to see you."

"Oh?"

"Seated right over there, the young lady in the blue dress."

He looked in the direction indicated and saw the lady, who had seen the motions and had stood. She was taller than average, perhaps five feet seven inches. She had long brown hair and he bet brown gorgeous eyes. She walked quickly to where he stood and held out her hand.

"You must be Canyon O'Grady. Mr. Priestly said I could find you here. My name is Lacey Eckstrom, that's U.S. Agent Eckstrom."

He had taken her hand but dropped it when she said who she was.

"I told Mr. Priestly that I work alone. I don't need any help. And since when do we have women U.S. agents?"

"As of three months ago, Mr. O'Grady. You haven't been reading your communications. As far as working with someone on this job, Mr. O'Grady, I told Mr. Priestly the same thing: I don't need any help. I'm a qualified U.S. agent assigned to Justice. Yes, I'm the first woman agent. Does that bother you, Mr. O'Grady?"

"Yes, it bothers me just one hell of a lot. Where can we talk? I was about to have some supper, would you join me? Of course, since you're a U.S. agent, you'll have to pay for your own."

"I fully intended to, Mr. O'Grady. I wouldn't dream of taking a favor of any kind from you."

A short time later they were seated in the hotel dining room; they had ordered, and Canyon O'Grady held his temper in check. He was furious at Priestly.

"Before you start spouting off where my proper place as a woman is, let me give you some facts. I shoot ninety-eight out of a hundred on the short-weapon firing range. I have done research for two years under a Supreme Court justice and graduated from college with a bachelor's degree in criminal law. I have two years' experience in the Washington, D.C., police force as a special investigator, and now I'm a qualified United States agent.''

She took a deep breath. "I'm here not because I asked for the job, nor because I wanted it, but because President Buchanan ordered me here to work with you on the assassination plot."

"Oh, damn," O'Grady said softly.

Lacey grinned. "So, neither one of us has much to say about our assignments. We could quit, of course, and get bounced right out of the service. But I'm staying and will make the best of a bad situation. Any rebuttal?"

"This isn't some damned college debate. I wish it were. So, I'm stuck with you. Please stay out of my way and you'll cause us both as few problems as possible."

Lacey laughed without mirth. "Mr. O'Grady, you're the one who should stay out of the way. I've been working on this case in our Washington office since we first heard of it almost six weeks ago. I've been the one to tie down the sources, verify them, and at last figure out who the actual perpetrators might be. Don't get condescending with me or I'll punch you right in the eye."

The soup course came then and Canyon settled back while the waitress served them. When she was gone, he stared at Lacey. "So you've done some good work, so far. But remember that was office work. Now we're in the field, where the bad guys don't look at us from a sheet of paper; they shoot back. Have you ever been shot at, Miss Eckstrom?" Her eyes widened and her mouth came open in a silent oh. "No, I can see that you haven't been. That's what happens in the field. I was shot at several times this morning. To bring you up to date, Dade Matzner, one of Nymon's Raiders, is now in jail in La Salle ten miles west of here. He's being held on a murder and bank-robbery charge. The local sheriff and some deputies from La Salle and myself captured him this morning and fired at the other three. Yes, and Marcella Quiney is riding with them this time, on a horse, sidesaddle.''

She looked up, her hand holding a spoon. There was surprise and some admiration showing in her brown eyes. For the first time there was a hint of a smile. ''You don't waste any time. Maybe I misjudged you, O'Grady. I figured you were all Irish blarney and blow. I might have been wrong. Now, can we eat? I'm starving and the soup is getting cold.''

''One more thing. You might shoot well at a paper target. But have you ever aimed your weapon at another human being, let alone pulled the trigger and tried to kill him?'' O'Grady watched her for a moment. ''Think about that, Miss Crackerjack Agent, while you eat your soup,'' he said. For the first time he took a good look at her. Besides being tall, she was slender with good breasts and a long, elegant neck. Her face could be pretty when she smiled, and her complexion was flawless, eyes wavering pools of brown that now looked down at her soup. She started eating without looking up.

''You *are* hungry.''

She finished the soup before she glanced at him. ''At home there were five kids, and if you talked during a meal, you got that much less to eat. Bad habit I picked up, but it keeps me from going hungry. Oh, you don't have to brief me. I've read everything Priestly gave you. Fact is, I wrote most of it. Now, how do we split up the work?''

O'Grady was getting uncomfortable. He didn't want this pretty girl tagging along with him. He didn't want her around, period. But what could he do to get rid of her? He shrugged.

"Miss Eckstrom. I don't have an agenda or a list of little jobs to get done. I'm here to try to find some killers. They don't play hide-and-seek. They kill people for a living. It gets downright dangerous at times.

"I don't care what Priestly or the president told you. I work alone. All you have to do is sit in your hotel room and wave at people out the window and come down three times a day for meals. You might even hire a bathtub now and then if it pleases you. One thing I'm damn certain of: you better not get in my way or mess up anything I'm working on. I hope that's perfectly clear."

Her face worked. Her anger almost boiled over. Then she got control of herself and stood politely. In one swift movement she reached down and dumped his nearly full bowl of soup in his lap, turned, and marched out of the dining room.

O'Grady sputtered a moment, then was relieved that the soup wasn't all that hot anymore. He lifted the soup bowl back to the table, covered his wet trousers with a linen napkin, and sat there waiting for the rest of his supper.

His first impulse had been to bellow at her in rage and run after her, catch her, and give her a spanking over his knee like the spoiled child she was. But that emotion quickly faded, and by the time he got the soup bowl back on the table and mopped up what he could with her napkin, the shock had worn off. He slid his chair closer to the table and started to chuckle. Quite a lass they had sent to him. Quite a lass at that. But not one to upset him. He had a job to do and he'd get it done in spite of one Lacey Eckstrom, U.S. Agent.

By the time his roast-beef dinner arrived, he was trying to work out some of that agenda he told Lacey he didn't have. What the hell should he do next and how could he find the Nymon gang? He'd go check at the Willoughby Inn, an old-fashioned inn at the far edge of town. Forty years ago, before the trains came, it had been Ottawa's original overnight stop for stage riders.

It was too much to hope that the Nymon gang would be staying there and waiting for the debate day to come. They had the best part of two weeks. They could hit another bank before then, or perhaps just relax in some camp along a quiet stream. He'd do some exploration on horseback as well.

Tomorrow he'd rent a good horse and saddle and get started on his roundabouts. It was wishing for too much luck that he would find them.

No, he'd had his lucky day when Nymon took the bank down so close by and then failed in a clean getaway. One man caught and three more in the gang to nail.

That's when he thought of something else. Lincoln's rented house burned to the ground last night. Last night Nymon and his band of killers were eight miles west of Ottawa having just robbed a bank. Nymon couldn't have had anything to do with burning the house.

Did that mean there were two groups interested in killing the candidate for the U.S. Senate, Abraham Lincoln?

5

Three men sat huddled around a single kerosene lamp in the dark basement of the Ottawa Hardware Store. The wick was low and the shadows flickered on the men's faces from the wavering light.

"So what do we try tonight?" the shortest of the three men asked. His name was Kirk and he owned the store. He was a good family man, a pillar of the community. Kirk wore a full beard closely trimmed to half an inch by his wife every week. His hair and beard were jet black, which gave his light-blue eyes an even lighter hue.

"Told you the damn fire was a bad idea," a larger man sitting beside him said. He gripped a bottle of beer and tipped it as soon as he had spoken, and set it down with an unsteady hand. He went by the name of Pike. He had a three-day growth of stubble. Pike was nearly six feet tall, sturdy, the town's blacksmith when he worked at it.

"We can't do a damned thing if we're all drunk," the third man snapped. His name was Barnaby and he wore a jacket and tie, which made him seriously over-dressed for the gathering. "The fire didn't scare him away. He just rented another house, and that big guy, Harvey, now sticks like glue to him." Barnaby was a lawyer and quick with his comments; he was medium height, five-seven. He smoothed down a pencil-line mustache and his dark eyes stared at the other two.

"I vote we use rifles," Barnaby said. "All three of us from three different spots. Say we get ready tonight, pick out our firing positions, and wait for him to come out the front door in the morning. One of us should be able to hit him from forty, fifty yards."

"I don't like rifles," Pike said.

"Pike, when you're drunk, you don't like nothing but booze and unsavory women. Now, are we serious about this venture or not? If we don't get serious, I'm voiding the agreement and going home." Barnaby was a lawyer at all times.

"Hell, got to be done," Kirk said. "We all agreed on that. If he gets elected to the Senate he'll quit to run for the president sure as snake shit."

"Pike, you with us?" Barnaby asked.

"Hell, yes. I know my duty."

"Then let's go take a look at his new rented house and pick out our spots while it's still light. He and his people rented the old Johnson place just down from the post office and up from the livery barn."

"Dammit to hell," Kirk said. "Wish somebody else would do it."

"You know nobody is gonna, Kirk," Barnaby said. "It's up to us, like it always was. Let's get on with it. But let's not go all together. We walk one by one up to where we can see the place; one goes on by, the other turns down one street, and the last man turns the other way. Then we meet back here and compare notes. Pick out two spots you can use to fire from. That way we'll work out any overlapping."

"Yeah, yeah, we can see that," Kirk said.

They returned a half-hour later through the back door of the hardware and went down to the basement, where the black powder was kept. It was also the new headquarters of the Defeat A. Lincoln Committee.

Kirk spoke first. "Found the ideal spot," he said.

"Three doors down on the other side of the street is that old house that the well-driller took over. It's got a false front on it and a loose board I can shoot out of. Not over forty yards."

Barnaby went next. "Just across Center Street three houses down from Lincoln's, I found this old maple tree that's all grown up to suckers. Plenty of room in there to hide and get off a good shot. Maybe thirty-five yards away."

"Found me a wagon that's sitting on same side of the street three houses down from the Johnson place," Pike said. "It's got some sacks of wheat in it and has a tarp over it. I'll be under the tarp with a good shot on anybody coming out the front door."

"Be too dark at night to be sure we get the right man," Barnaby said. "We don't want to make any mistakes now. Let's all get some sleep and go to our spots at four A.M. Nobody'll be on the streets by then."

Kirk nodded. "So we track anybody coming out of that house in the morning. When that tall son of a bitch shows his head outside, we shoot it off his shoulders! Go for the chest, a lot more sure to get a hit."

Barnaby looked at the other two. "You both have fired your rifles recently?" They nodded. "No need to worry about a second shot. If we can't do it with three shots, we won't have a chance to load. Wait for a clear shot. If Harvey comes out with him, wait for him to leave or go get a buggy or something.

"But be ready. As soon as one of us fires, the other two have to get off their own shots damn fast. We better not be seen together anymore for a while. I've got an appointment at my law office. I'll go out the alley to the north."

Barnaby waved and went to the back door of the store, slipped out, and walked out to the street and down half a block on Center Street to Main. His office was over the saddle shop in midblock on Main to the north.

A man came into his office less than a minute after Barnaby arrived. The man, tall and thin, pushed up a hat that half covered his face.

"Mr. Alacron," Barnaby said, surprised. "I thought we agreed you would never come here."

"Did, but we have an emergency. There's a federal agent in town with news that some foreign power is trying to kill Senator Douglas. You're not double-crossing me, are you, Barnaby?"

"Absolutely not. You've known me for ten years. We can't let Lincoln get into the Senate and use that as a stepping-stone to the presidency. His slavery views would split the country and ruin both of us."

"All right. The federal man wasn't sure if it was our man or Lincoln these foreign agents would try to kill. They'll be using American outlaws for the job, so it won't be anything clever or stylish. Maybe even from horseback. I want you to be damn sure that you watch our backside for any such gang."

"You bet, Mr. Alacron. But after tomorrow there won't be any debates, because there won't be any Lincoln. We're working a plan."

"I don't want to know about it. But I hope it works better than the damn sloppy fire you started. You should have gone inside and knocked out Lincoln first or bashed his head in and then started the fire."

"Don't worry, tomorrow morning it will be all over. If there's no debate, Senator Douglas can go back to the capitol at Springfield and play politics in tight security."

"It better be good, this surprise for Lincoln. Now, can I get out of here down the back stairs?"

Barnaby let him out and then sat behind his desk. Tomorrow morning he had to do it. With Lincoln dead, those foreign agents might change their plans. Maybe they were really going after Lincoln, and not Douglas. It was possible.

There was plenty of time for him to get home and check on the rifle he kept there. It was long and heavy and shot as straight as a ramrod. Barnaby grinned just thinking about tomorrow morning.

Several blocks up the street, Marcella Quiney sat in the town's only real hotel, the Plainsman. She had registered a few hours ago after a hard ride in from the west, then had taken a glorious hot bath in her room and dressed for supper and the evening.

She had on a delicious green dress that had cost a fortune in St. Louis. It swept the floor decorously, nipped in her waist even more, and let her bosom swell with interesting cleavage. It was nearly a party dress, but she was determined to have a party tonight even if she had to invite her own guests. Her blond hair was stacked high on her head to make her look taller, and she wore three-inch spike heels to help promote the same fiction.

She was reading in a leather-bound volume of *Leaves of Grass* by Walt Whitman when she saw the man she had been waiting for come in. Marcella stood rapidly and hurried toward the stairs in the same direction the man was going. At the precise moment she wanted to, she stumbled, dropped her book, and threw out her hands, but she couldn't stop herself. She slammed into the man and they both tumbled to the floor. Her skirts hiked up to her knees and one breast nearly popped out of her tight bodice.

She sat up pretending to be groggy. She shook her head as if to clear it and the man brushed her skirt down to cover her legs.

"Oh, gracious! What happened?" she asked in an

accent-free voice she had mastered. It even had a bit of a New England twang to it. She blinked and looked at the man on the floor beside her. "Was I clumsy again and ran into you?" she asked in a small apologetic voice. Her sparkling green eyes looked over at him and Canyon O'Grady returned the stare.

For a moment he was serious, then he grinned. "I'm not sure who ran into who, miss. I was thinking about something and rushing to get to my room. My most humble apologies. Let me help you up."

He stood gracefully and lifted her to her feet. He noticed at once that she was a tiny thing, but that did not describe her bosom and the delightful cleavage he saw there. She brushed off her green skirt and he stood there transfixed. He was glad she wasn't a redhead and didn't have a southern accent.

"I'm sorry I crashed into you, miss. My name is Canyon O'Grady. Can I help you to a chair or get you a glass of water or a bottle of liniment?"

She laughed, and he enjoyed hearing it.

"Thank you, Mr. O'Grady. I'm fine. I don't bruise easily. I was really on my way to the dining room. I'm absolutely famished." She left it hanging there, and there was little else a gentleman could do. Not that he minded in the least.

"Would you allow me to escort you to supper? It's nearly time, and I'm told they serve some of the best food in town here. Not exactly Delmonico's in New York, but really quite good."

She looked up and frowned for a moment. "But we've not even met. It doesn't sound proper."

He took her hand and led her to the hotel clerk, who had seen the collision and seemed relieved that there were no broken bones and no bloodshed.

"Sir," O'Grady said to the clerk, "my name is Canyon O'Grady. I'd appreciate it if you could formally introduce me to this delightful young lady who just knocked me down."

She laughed softly and whispered something to the clerk.

"Mr. Canyon O'Grady, it is my distinct pleasure to introduce you to Miss Mary Jane Fillmore, of New York City." He looked at them both. "Miss Fillmore, Mr. O'Grady. Mr. O'Grady, Miss Fillmore."

O'Grady handed the clerk a dollar bill and held out his arm for the girl. "Now that we've been formally introduced, Miss Mary Jane Fillmore, would you do me the honor of accepting my invitation to supper?"

She grinned, an impish, half-taunting expression that made him want to reach down and kiss her. "Mr. O'Grady. Even though you're Irish and my old father warned me against the Irish, I'll be happy to have supper with you."

"Shall we?" He held out his arm and she took it and they walked into the dining room at the Plainsman Hotel.

It was a delightful meal, but afterward, O'Grady could hardly remember what they ate. When supper was over, he paid the bill and they walked out to the lobby.

"I do need to go to my room," she said.

"As we said during supper, there should be an opera or at least a symphony to attend since you're so dressed up, but I'm afraid there isn't much here to do after dark."

"We could play cards in the lobby," she said.

They walked toward the stairway, and up. Her room was on the second floor, number 214.

She stopped and twisted a key in the lock. "I don't suppose . . ." She sighed and shook her head. "No, not possible." She pushed the door open and stood there watching him. "I do have a bottle of brandy and some cards," she said in a rush. "Oh, dear!"

He waited, smiling.

"If you would care to . . . I mean, I know it's forward, but I just thought . . . We could have a small glass of brandy and play some gin rummy, or something."

"We could leave the door partly open," O'Grady said. "I would be enthralled to play some cards with you." He paused. "Do you have any people here? I mean, we don't want to do anything that might hurt your reputation."

She smiled. "I'm traveling alone and was set to stay only the night before going south to pick up the train for Omaha. I'm on my way to San Francisco."

She looked up at him plaintively, then that wicked little smile came and slanted away. "Yes, Mr. O'Grady. I'm a grown woman. I can do what I please. Come in, we'll have a touch of brandy and then play some cards. Nobody here knows me, and even if they did, I'd say fie on them!" She stepped inside and O'Grady went in behind her. He left the door ajar about six inches. The room was much like his just down the hallway, also on the second floor.

For the briefest moment he wondered where Lacey Eckstrom was staying. The thought flashed away as Mary Jane turned. The smile on her face made him forget everything else.

"I've got the brandy right here. I even carry two small glasses for emergencies just like this. A medical emergency, a touch of brandy to soothe our physical pain after that fall downstairs."

O'Grady smiled. "Yes, Dr. Mary Jane. I think that would be just the right medicine."

6

Mary Jane Fillmore took a small flask from her traveling case and a pair of small glasses and poured them each two fingers of the brandy. He took a sip. It was good.

"You have an excellent taste in brandy, Miss Fillmore," O'Grady said.

"My bringing-up. Now, for some cards." She looked around the room. "The only place to play is . . . on the bed." She took a long breath. "You sit down there on the side and I'll sit here, and we can use the bed between us as our card table."

They sat down and she dealt out a hand of gin rummy, then picked up her cards and sorted them quickly.

"You've played before," he said.

"Now and then. I can't learn to play that new game, bridge."

Mary Jane won the first three hands. "We're playing for a prize," she said as she won the third hand. "I forgot to tell you that when we started. The winner of three hands gets to have a prize from the other person. I won three hands."

"Sounds fair to me. What's your prize?"

She smiled, then looked away. "The prize I want from you is a soft, gentle kiss." She looked up. "Are you shocked?"

"Surprised maybe, not shocked."

She leaned toward him and their lips barely met, and then she pulled back. "No, no, that's not a kiss. You come up here and let me kiss you."

He moved past the cards and sat on the bed next to her. She put her arms around him and her lips met his fully, seriously, then parted slightly. Slowly she fell backward on the bed and pulled him with her until he lay half on top of her.

Her mouth was fully open now, her tongue working at his lips, which parted, and her hot tongue darted into his mouth, eager, searching. Her breasts pushed hard against his chest and he could feel their heat and the beat of her heart through the twin mounds of flesh crushed against him.

Slowly she pulled back from his lips, her green eyes sparkling. She watched him a minute, then pushed him away slightly so she could focus on him.

"Oh, Canyon! That was about the best kiss I've ever had. I think it's only fair now that I kiss back, don't you think? I mean, just to be fair about this."

He nodded and she reached up and kissed him again, this time her mouth fully open, her eyes closed. She caught one of his hands and pulled it between them so it lay on her breasts. Their tongues fought this time and his hand softly rubbed her breasts, working over from the cleavage to the ripeness of her surging mounds. He found a nipple and tweaked it and rubbed it back and forth, feeling it harden and surge larger with an influx of fresh blood.

She ended the kiss and watched him from her green cat eyes.

"Canyon O'Grady, you are a wonderful kisser." She smiled. "I like the way your hand knows just where to go and how to make me feel even better. Could you do me a favor? Please move over and close the door and turn the key in the lock. We don't need anyone coming in here by mistake.''

He lifted away from her and locked the door. When he turned back to her, she had unfastened the front of the green dress and held out the sides.

"Pull them down a little, I'm feeling all cramped inside this old dress."

He tugged down the top and her breasts surged out, starkly white with pink nipples and lighter areolae three inches wide.

"Beautiful," he whispered.

"You could be polite and at least say hello to them with a kiss."

He bent and kissed both, working around them one at a time until he reached the very tip, where he chewed on her nipple tenderly and then pulled the orb into his mouth.

Gently she pushed him down on the bed on his back and hung over him, dropping a breast into his open mouth.

"Canyon O'Grady, I wanted you to kiss me the first time you knocked me down out there in the lobby. Wasn't that silly? I didn't know you or nothing."

He couldn't answer, his mouth was full. He caught her hand and moved it down to his fly, where there was a serious swelling. He sat up and slowly began to unbutton and unsnap her dress. She helped, and a moment later stood and pulled the green garment off over her head. There was no chemise, since the dress was cut so low. Now her bare breasts thrust out as she stood there and he bent and kissed them again. She had several petticoats on.

"You next," she said, and pushed back his suit coat and took it off. Then she unbuttoned his shirt. He helped, and soon it came off as well. She smiled as she ran her fingers through the copper hair on his chest.

"Redheads are my favorite," she said. "Just so manly and so sexy."

He caught at her petticoats and she slipped them off all at once, three of them; she wore only some loose-fitting cotton short drawers. She tugged at his belt and unbuttoned his fly, and then went down and pulled his boots off and then his pants.

"You first," she said. He stripped down his underwear and she squealed as she saw his penis, ramrod-hard and slanting out toward her. She bent and caught it and then kissed the very tip and watched his hips jerk.

He put his hands on her hips and pulled down her drawers to show a reddish muff.

They stretched out together on the bed and she rolled on top of him and stared into his eyes.

"I'm not sure how this happened so fast. I mean, I don't want you to think that I let just anyone . . . you know, take off my clothes this way. You're something special. I knew that first time I saw you." His hands caressed her body, from her legs all the way up to her shoulder blades and then back down. She sighed and purred. "I feel like a well-fed, wanted pussy cat," she said, nibbling at his ear.

"Good, because you are wanted."

She smiled. "God, I hope so. I'd hate to have to out and out rape you at this point."

"No danger."

He rolled her off him, parted her knees, and went between them on his knees. He massaged her muff and her wet outer lips with one hand as he leaned forward and kissed her lips gently.

"The first time, soft and easy and slow, like I'm a virgin, please?"

He nodded. Her juices were flowing, and he entered

53

her gently, then worked in until they were impaled on each other pelvic bone to bone.

"Delicious! You are delicious!" She trembled then and he reached between them, found her clit, and strummed it a dozen times, sending her into a series of five potent spasms that left her limp and panting.

"Oh, God, oh God. Nobody ever did that for me before. I mean, I've never been so nicely treated. You're special, Canyon O'Grady, and I'm gonna hate . . . gonna hate to have to go on to the train."

"You could stay here a few days. If you're short on money, you can stay in my room."

She didn't answer him. She just pushed him up and then tugged him forward so they pounded together.

"Do me good, Canyon! Hit me hard. Go just as fast and hard as you want to. I like it that way."

It had been a while and he was ready. O'Grady pounded at her and drove her up the bed as he hammered and hammered; then, before he could stop it, he exploded in one mind-shattering blast.

She put her arms around him. "You're so damn handsome and you're such a good fucker, whatever am I going to do with you?"

He was too exhausted to answer as the mini death hit him hard. She held him tightly. Her own hard breathing had come to an end. She hadn't climaxed again when he did. Some did, some didn't, he knew.

It was ten minutes before he wanted to talk. She kept him pinned tightly to her, her arms around his back. When he stirred, she let him go and they sat on the edge of the bed. He got the brandy and poured them another shot and they both sipped it instead of tossing it down.

"Brandy should be enjoyed," he told her.

She nodded, then leaned over and patted his shriveled-up worm and kissed his cheek. "Dear, sweet

Canyon. I want you to stay with me all night. Can you do that? I don't want to sleep alone after such a grand one. Maybe two or three or four more, do you think?''

He laughed and caught her face with one hand and turned it toward him. He kissed her pouting lips and then both eyes.

''Little darling Mary Jane, you couldn't get me out of your bed tonight with anything less than a sawed-off shotgun.''

''Good, good. Only trouble is we might run out of brandy.''

''We'll get by,'' he said. ''Somehow we'll get by.''

''You ready for number two?'' she asked, reaching toward his crotch.

''Mary Jane, you'll know when I'm ready.'' He pulled her on top of him and kissed her breasts.

It was some hours later when he woke up and looked at his big pocket watch in the low, soft glow of the lamp. It was just after two A.M. She woke up and smiled at him.

''No sense in wasting the rest of the night by sleeping. You said something about sidesaddle. What did you mean by that?''

He showed her the sidesaddle position for making love, and she laughed so hard they had to revert back to a more basic position. Then she wasn't laughing anymore. Her whole body stiffened in rapture as one blitzing set of tremors rattled through her, setting her to gasping and moaning and crying out in total joy until she collapsed and for a moment he thought she had passed out.

Then he was the one who couldn't hold back any longer, and he pounded into her as if he hadn't climaxed for six months.

That set her off again and they moaned and yelped and roared and slammed against each other in a panting jolting crescendo that left them both drained and unable to move.

They went to sleep in each other's arms and didn't wake up until just after daylight.

Canyon O'Grady came upright in the bed, his eyes staring out the window, which they had opened sometime during the night. The lamp still burned, but it looked low and feeble now in the daylight.

"What was that?" O'Grady asked.

Mary Jane slept on.

He eased out of bed and looked out the window. He heard it again, this time he knew what it was. Somebody had fired a rifle, then a half a minute later the third shot came.

O'Grady pulled on his pants. This was not a wildwest town. He hadn't seen a single man carrying a gun except a law officer since he got here, except Nymon's Raiders.

Dammit, he was sure that the Nymon gang wouldn't try for the men until the day of the big debate. Had that mistake cost a man's life?

He pulled on his shirt and jacket, but he didn't bother with his tie as he ran out the door and hurried down the steps. When he got to the street, he saw two men running to the north. He followed them.

"What's going on?" he called.

"Heard a couple of rifle shots, up this way. Ain't heard a shot in town for five years."

"Damn," Canyon O'Grady said, and ran past the man toward a small group of men around the house where he had talked to Abraham Lincoln's campaign manager. A body lay half in and half out of the front door. It wasn't moving.

7

Three men hovered over the man sprawled in the open front doorway.

O'Grady rushed up and edged in past one man and looked at the wounded man's face. He was not Mr. Lincoln. "Who is he?" O'Grady asked.

"Don't know," a man in a soft cap said. "I was just going down to work and I heard two shots and this guy fell."

"See who did the shooting?"

"No, but they caught somebody running away. Some guy was hiding in that parked wagon down there."

"Good."

The man on the floor groaned.

"Where are you hit, mister?" O'Grady asked. He asked it again, and the man blinked his eyes open and looked up.

"My leg. Hurts like hell."

"Who are you?" O'Grady asked.

"Harvey. I work for Mr. Lincoln."

"We need a doctor," O'Grady said. He looked at one of the men. "Do you live here? Know where the doctor lives?"

"Right," the man in the soft cap said. "I'll go fetch him."

Another man ran up with a pistol out. He was one

of the sheriff's deputies. The deputy recognized O'Grady.

"All yours, Deputy," Canyon said. "There's a suspect down there somewhere. I'll go find him."

Down the street, two men had a larger man pinned against a farm wagon. A rifle lay at his feet. One of the men had a three-foot two-by-four he waved at the tall man beside the wagon.

O'Grady looked at the three. "This the man who did the bushwhacking?"

"One of them," the man without the club said. "I heard three shots. One from the wagon here. Two more up the street. This one tried to sneak out, but we grabbed him."

"Know who he is?"

"Name's Pike Rauscher. He's the town's blacksmith when he ain't drunk, which is maybe about half the time."

"Hold him for the sheriff. Good work." O'Grady ambled back toward the Lincoln house. Pike was local, he couldn't be in with the Nymon gang. He wouldn't last half a minute with them. So what was this all about?

By the time O'Grady got back to the victim, the doctor had arrived and was instructing two men to carry Harvey down to his medical office.

Sheriff Tillery ran up and talked with his deputy, then looked at O'Grady. "How come you got here first, O'Grady?"

"Guess I put on my pants faster than you do, Sheriff. Harvey say how many shots he heard?"

"Three. That one of the gunmen down there by the wagon?"

"He is, if the man with the two-by-four doesn't bash his brains out before you get there. His name's Pike."

"Pike, the blacksmith?" the sheriff asked. "Don't sound right."

"Looks like they were trying for Mr. Lincoln. One of them mistook Harvey there for him. Good thing none of them was a good shot. Damn, this can't be the Nymon gang. You say Pike's local?"

"Yeah, but he don't have brains enough to figure out something like this. He was the only one caught?"

"Afraid so."

The sheriff headed for Pike.

O'Grady saw a woman down by the wagon but paid her no attention. How in hell did this fit in with the Nymon threat? Or did it? He needed some breakfast. He always thought better when he had a full stomach.

He headed toward the hotel, and as he did, he thought of Mary Jane Fillmore. What a pretty little package. What a sexy little bundle. She just could never seem to get enough. He hoped that she stayed around for a while. At least she wasn't southern, no accent, no red hair.

He was almost to the Plainsman Hotel when he noticed that someone was trying to catch up with him. He looked quickly that way and realized with a start that he had no weapon. His hideout derringer was in the hotel along with his gun belt and .45 revolver.

With a touch of relief he noted it was a woman and that she was Lacey Eckstrom, the U.S. agent.

"You're up early, O'Grady," Lacey said.

"I heard the shots."

"Me too. Evidently someone tried to kill Mr. Lincoln but picked the wrong man. Did you talk to Mr. Weaver, the man with the two-by-four?"

"A little. Why?"

"Then you probably heard that Pike is a drunk and a hanger-on, and doesn't have a thought in his head."

"So why did he try to shoot Mr. Lincoln?"

"That's what Mr. Weaver and I talked about. Seems Pike does a tolerable bit of his drinking with a man named Kirk, who runs the Ottawa Hardware. Kirk used to be in politics. Was in the state legislature for a time, now a dyed-in-the-wool Democrat and a strong man to maintain the status quo."

"You learn a lot in a short time. The man shot in the leg was named Harvey; he's evidently a body guard for the candidate."

"Pike's rifle had been fired."

"I could smell the smoke from the black powder when I talked to him." O'Grady hesitated. They were at the hotel. "You hungry? Be nice and I'll buy you breakfast."

"No, I'm in no mood to be nice, so let me buy *you* breakfast. I went to see you in your room last night. You weren't there."

"Must have missed me."

"I missed you all night, or at least until about one A.M., when I gave up."

"I was busy."

"I know. I saw you come running out of a room down the hall this morning. I also checked up on Mary Jane Fillmore. At least that's the name she registered with at the desk."

Canyon looked at her quickly, his face set as he tried to control his sudden anger. "You have no right to dig into—"

"The 'lady' registered yesterday. I had a talk with her in the lobby. The fact is she was waiting for someone, and that someone turned out to be you. She saw you come in. She quickly moved toward you, and when you looked away, she fell into you quite deliberately and with enough skill and practice to knock you both to the floor."

"You don't know any of this."

"Oh, but I do. It's the same technique I used to strike up a conversation with a suspect. Although I didn't wind up in his bed."

"You—"

"O'Grady, I'm sorry, I didn't mean to say that. Your private life is certainly no concern of mine. But I think you should know that the lady is now a blonde, but hasn't been for long. There are red roots showing on her blond hair."

"She doesn't have a southern accent."

"Honey chile, what you all want a girl to sound like just so she can be a suthun belle?" Lacey said the words with a thick down-South accent. "Any actress can put on or keep off an accent at the drop of a casting call. What I'm saying is that this Mary Jane is quite probably Marcella Quiney, who would have no qualms at all about using her feminine charms on you to see if you're a threat to Nymon's Raiders."

O'Grady remembered Mary Jane's red muff, and that made him all the madder. "Miss Eckstrom, you really weren't hungry, were you? I'm not hungry at all." He turned at the door to the hotel and went inside and marched up to his room. There he dug out his sidearm and strapped on the heavy belt. He made sure the weapon was loaded with five charges, settled it into place on his hip, and tied down the lower end of the holster around his leg with a leather thong.

Then he went downstairs to have breakfast, but he sat at the other end of the room from Agent Eckstrom. Damn her! Mostly damn her for probably being right about Mary Jane. She could have shot him with her derringer a half-dozen times last night. Which proved she wasn't sure who he was or what threat he might be. Evidently she didn't get a good look at him when the riders thundered past him yesterday morning out toward La Salle. Damn good thing. The ham and eggs didn't taste as good as they should.

After breakfast he went to the Willoughby Inn. There were only three guests checked in, and all had stayed there before many times over the years. None of them could be with the Nymon gang. Also, none of them looked like an international conspirator involved in a political assassination.

Since the Pike attack obviously had nothing to do with Nymon . . . Where was the bastard, anyway? O'Grady tried to put himself in the outlaw's shoes. He had just robbed a bank; he and Hoke must have at least a thousand dollars each. What would they do? Go to a town and stay at a hotel? Not Ottawa. The authorities would be on the lookout there. Another town? Perhaps. Should Canyon check around at hotels in other towns?

But if Mary Jane was really Marcella Quiney, had Nymon sent her into town to test the waters?

Maybe they were camped out along a stream somewhere sleeping away the days in the sun and living a good life. It would be better for Nymon if Marcella was along. What a wild tiger she was in bed.

O'Grady knew he couldn't give her another chance to kill him, but what did he do if she showed up in his room? He couldn't just boot her out or have her arrested. First, he had nothing to charge her with. Besides, he didn't want to alert Nymon the authorities knew he might be connected with a much bigger plot than a bank robbery.

O'Grady walked down to the livery stables and rented a horse. He found a deep-chested sorrel with a blaze on its forehead he liked. He rented a saddle as well and went on a getting-acquainted ride.

The mount was strong, responsive, and liked to run. Canyon headed out along the Illinois River. He rode for two miles, skirted the heavier brush, and checked in some of the likely-looking camping spots, but he failed to see any smoke or any vestiges of campfires. On the way back he swung away from the river and worked through the open country, but was surprised how much settlement there was. Some of the fields were fenced, many had been put to the plow and had been harvested. He saw where wheat or oats had been grown and two fields where hay had been cut and winnowed. Civilization was catching up with them even here in Illinois.

Back at the stable O'Grady told the hostler he was satisfied with the sorrel. Canyon wiped it down and put it in a stall. "I want the sorrel available at any time," he told the stable boy. He left the saddle on a sawhorse out front and walked down to the county sheriff's office.

Sheriff Tillery pulled at his sagging jowls from habit and walked around his office.

"Consarn it, O'Grady. I don't know what to make out of this shot that Pike took. He's usually not that interested in politics. Pounds a good anvil, drinks up a storm, and that's about it."

"Maybe he fell in with a bad crowd," O'Grady said.

"His usual crowd is a pint of beer and some peanuts at the local tavern."

"I hear he's a good friend of the hardware-store man, Kirk."

"Yeah, true, but Kirk is a shrimp who worries about getting the quarter-inch nuts on the quarter-inch bolts in time for inventory. Just don't figure."

"There were three shots. With those rifles there had to be three men and three weapons. Find your other men and you might have better luck figuring it."

"Might. We're charging Pike with attempted murder. Judge won't be around on the circuit for another three weeks. By then the damn debate will be over at least.''

"How is Harvey? He get patched up?''

"Yep. Good thing that aim wasn't higher. We'd be having a funeral. As it is, Sanborn is screaming for protection. He was down here right after he left the doctor's office and is demanding that we give Abe Lincoln some guards. Hell, I don't have enough men to do that. Told him this was a small town in a small county. He went off ranting about something.''

"Got to thinking, Sheriff Tillery. Maybe this Pike bunch isn't much of a threat. Looks like they bumbled a sure thing. Three high-powered rifles at thirty-five yards more or less. That's like shooting whales in a teacup, damn hard to miss. Yet all three men fired and all three missed. At least missed the target.

"Moreover, they picked out the wrong man to shoot at. At least one of them did. When that first man fired, the other two had to fire as well or fade into the bushes.''

"Yeah, hope to hell you're right, O'Grady. If not we have not one but two bunches trying to kill somebody. Make that trying to kill a U.S. senator and a nobody. Damn, I may be getting too long of tooth for this job.''

"I'm not applying for the position,'' O'Grady said, and stood. He waved at the sheriff and walked outside.

As he closed the door, a rider galloped down the middle of Main Street, scattering citizens and horses. The man came sliding to a stop at the sheriff's office, jumped off his lathered mount, and ran inside.

O'Grady was right behind him.

"Not more than an hour ago, Sheriff,'' the rider panted. "I saw them two bank robbers come out of the bank myself. Had masks on and sacks of money and shot at anybody they saw. Hear they killed some-

64

body inside. Being the only deputy in Cottonwood Bar, I got my horse and come riding out here damn fast. Knew you'd want to know.''

"Let's ride," Sheriff Tillery said, including O'Grady in his order.

3

Flint Nymon leaned back in a chair outside the hardware store in the small village of Cottonwood Bar and
watched the Illinois River swirl by a few feet away.
The little town had once been larger than it was now.
Once it had been a fording point for the river. Now
there was a bridge a few miles farther downstream.

Nymon watched the water, but most of his attention
was on the bank across the street and down four stores:
the Cottonwood Bar Bank, J. Livingston, President.
He had looked it over before.

"Wish we had old Dade back," Nymon said. "Dade
was a little shit, but he knew how to work over bank
customers and tellers. Damn but he was good." He
saw a look of concern on the face of the big man who
sat beside him. "Come on, Crunch, no worry. We can
take this little cardboard box with one hand in our
pocket. Here we both got two good ones. About an
hour more and we'll pay them a visit."

He lowered his voice. "You got it right now,
Crunch? We go in, I yell and draw and you lock the
door and get any customers down on the floor. Right?"

"Ahhhhh, right, Flint, right. I can do that."

There was a grin on his big, blunt face. He had
moved up a notch in the gang, now he was number
two. It didn't worry Crunch at all that there were only
two in the gang now. Nymon had a self-imposed rule:

66

never try to rescue one of his men who had been captured by lawmen. Flint had tried it once and lost two more men. Now he let them rot in jail or hang. His men knew that.

A man walked down the street looking at the stores on both sides. He had a gun on his hip, which was unusual in this town. Then Nymon saw the tin badge on his chest. He grinned. Just might get himself a deputy sheriff or a marshal or whatever the man called himself here. Flint and Crunch had tied their horses in the alley just in back of the bank. They had spent the morning buying some provisions and getting ready for a ride and a camp-out.

Marcella should have her work done in town in another day and would meet them in that dense little woods they had discovered riding away from that damn posse. He'd underestimated that lawman. Sheriffs in this part of the country weren't supposed to be that smart. Nymon shrugged. He was just glad it hadn't been him who drew the luck of the lawman's bullet.

Old Dade was still alive, last he had seen. Probably have to stand trial in that little town for murder and bank robbery. Way it happened. Nobody's fault, things just happen.

He shifted on the chair and stood.

"Time, Crunch. Let's go see what we can find in the gentleman's bank over there."

Since no one in the small town wore guns on their hips, neither did Nymon and Crunch. They had them inside their shirts, and handy.

When Nymon stepped into the bank, there were three customers—two women and a man—and two tellers and the president. Flint walked up to the teller and pushed the other two people aside waiting in line.

"Now, Crunch," he boomed, and Hoke threw the bolt in the outside door and jumped and grabbed the man and one of the women customers and pushed them down on the floor.

The big six-gun jolted out of Nymon's shirt into his hand and he waved it at the teller.

"This here's a holdup, young feller. Lace your fingers together on top your head. You too," Nymon barked the last order at the second teller, who had been reaching for a gun.

The bank president was partly shielded by a partition and his desk. He dropped to the floor behind the desk and pulled a revolver out of the lower drawer and edged it over the back of the desk. When his head came up high enough so he could see, Nymon blew the top of it off with a well-placed .45 round. The slug went in the banker's forehead, jolted straight through, and carried a four-inch square of skull, brains, and gray matter with it as it sped out of the man's head.

As the crashing sound of the big .45 revolver round faded away, Crunch had the second woman flat on the floor. He frisked the man but found no weapon.

Nymon vaulted over the counter and pushed the tellers out of the way. He scooped up the money in their drawers, found the extra supply in the small drawer below the counter, and dropped all the paper and gold coins into a leather bag he carried.

When he had the second teller's cage cleared out, he shoved both tellers toward the vault.

"Well, the door's open, that's very thoughtful and nice of you boys. Get all the cash in the vault and put it into this bag, fast. We don't have a lot of time."

The tellers began to move stacks of bills into the bag.

Nymon roared in anger and slashed the heavy revolver down across the face of one of the young men, tearing the side of his eye down and ripping away part of his nose. The teller slumped to the floor unconscious.

"All the money, bastard," Nymon shouted. "Don't go leaving any of it like that jackass did."

Two minutes later the bank's total supply of cash was in the leather bag.

Nymon looked at the younger of the two women on the floor. "What's the matter, sweetheart?" he asked, squatting down beside her. He lifted her chin with his hand. "Hey, you don't have to be afraid. I'm not going to hurt anybody as pretty as you." He lifted her up to a sitting position and pushed his hand down to her breasts. "Oh, my, yes, good tits." He fondled them. "You married?" She shook her head.

Someone knocked on the locked front door of the bank.

"Too damn bad we don't have more time, sweet tits. We could do us some funning." Nymon whirled, saw the clerk bringing up a revolver he had taken from a hiding place in the vault. The big .45 in Nymon's hand roared again and the teller with the heavy handgun took the round in his chest and slammed backward into the vault on top of his unconscious friend.

"Out," Nymon said. The two men backed toward the rear door. Crunch opened it and looked outside. He nodded. Then they both were out and running down the alley to their horses.

The man customer on the floor made sure the killers were gone, then he ran to the front door, unbolted it, and rushed out screaming that there had been a bank robbery.

Deputy Sheriff Yancy Ronset had been on First Street checking on a broken window in the back of the hardware store when he saw the two men running down the alley. One had a canvas bag, but that was not unusual.

The taller man turned and fired a quick pistol shot at Ronset. He ducked behind a building, drew his revolver, and fired twice at the two men as they mounted and rode on out the alley. They had been out of range, but he fired anyway.

A moment later he heard the scream from Main Street about the bank robbery and headed for the street and his horse. He went through the bank, saw the two dead men and the injured one, and ordered the first civilian he saw to run for Dr. Warnick. Then he grabbed his horse and began his five-mile ride to the sheriff's office over in Ottawa.

It took them a half-hour in Ottawa to get the posse raised, and O'Grady saddled his horse and rode with them. The two killers had ridden east out of Cottonwood Bar, but there was no telling how long they had kept going in that direction.

It took the posse another forty-five minutes to get to the bank, and by then the trail the robbers had taken out of town was over three hours old. The sheriff left one of his deputies to handle the cleanup at the bank, but kept the local man with him to help identify the robbers if that was needed.

A half-mile out of town the trail of the two riders evaporated. They had been heading east at a gallop for a quarter of a mile, then dropped to a walk down the main road along the river.

One of the sets of prints angled into the grass along the trail and then faded out. The other set veered across the trail into the grass on the far side and never came back.

O'Grady knelt down at the spot and saw faint traces of hoofprints and bootprints, but even those vanished after twenty more feet.

"They didn't just vanish," Sheriff Tillery brayed. "Where in hell did they go?"

"Boots," O'Grady said. "Had an outlaw in Colorado who used to do that. He'd ride out of town, stop in a grassy section, and tie padded boots around the horse's hooves. The horses hate them, but the animal can then walk through most grassy areas and you won't be able to track it. On a hard road like this, there has to be a lot of dust to set up a print of the pillow.''

"Who the hell thought of that?''

"Some cavalry officer trying to sneak up on Indians, as I recall,'' O'Grady said. "We won't find Nymon. Not from this track. Once they ride off a few miles, they take the boots off and there's no way to match any kind of prints by then.''

They rode back to town and talked to the eyewitnesses. The teller with the smashed face was little help. The young girl said she could identify both the killers, if she ever saw them again. She gave good descriptions of both and told how the smaller man had . . . made advances and actually touched her breast.

"We'll get them,'' Sheriff Tillery said.

O'Grady wasn't so sure. With the head start they had and the boots, they had gotten away completely. It would be happenchance to find them again. Unless they were waiting around near Ottawa for the big debate.

Canyon figured the little town's bank was dead and gone. With the president dead and all of its cash reserves gone, the heirs would have to decide what to do with whatever value there was left in mortgages, property, and perhaps some stocks. Everyone who had money in the bank would lose it. The whole little town might just curl up and die along with the bank.

O'Grady rode back to Ottawa with the posse. They arrived just before six o'clock. By the time he put his horse away and rubbed it down, Canyon was hungry enough to eat the left flank of his sorrel. He made it to the hotel, washed up, combed his red hair, and then went down for some supper.

Lacey Eckstrom was waiting for him.

"You again," O'Grady said.

"Tonight I'm going to buy you that supper you didn't want last night. I've got some news for you, but you don't get it quite yet. What happened in Cottonwood Bar?"

He told her about the robbery and murders, then they went in and sat down and ordered supper—his, steak and all the trimmings; hers, a chicken and lots of coffee.

"So what is Nymon doing, working at his usual trade until the time for the big mark here in town?" she asked.

"Looks that way. That Nymon has more nerve than a strutting turkey on Thanksgiving morning. But his time will come."

Lacey picked up a drumstick and took off a healthy bite. "Don't stare, O'Grady. I'm a farm girl and I know how to ride and how to eat chicken. I also had a long talk with the sheriff this morning while you were joyriding on your sorrel.

"We took Pike a fifth of whiskey. In another hour or two he should be talking his head off. Pike is a talker when he gets smashed, and he's not too good on whiskey. Should be an interesting evening."

"Is that your news?" O'Grady asked, taking another bite of the steak with his fork in his left hand.

"Part of it."

He watched her. She was an attractive woman. He'd never noticed that before. And she had a good figure, a little tall and lean for his druthers, but he was sure she would be a handful between the sheets. Not that he ever intended to find out.

"Part of your news?"

"Right. The rest is that your ladyfriend checked out this afternoon. My guess is that she was here to test the waters and see if there was any special security or any talk about someone aiming to hurt the debaters."

"She left on the train?" he asked.

"Matter of fact, she didn't. She hired a buggy and took off north on a trail of a road that leads into farm country."

"Farm country? Suppose she has kin up that way?"

"Doubt it, O'Grady."

"She's going to meet Nymon."

"About the size of it. I hired a horse and followed her."

O'Grady looked at the tall girl. "You did what?"

"I tailed her. Horse can go dang near anywhere a buggy can."

"She spot you?"

Lacey stared at him with the beginnings of anger.

"I'm sorry, you wouldn't let her see you. Know where she went?"

"Yes, a patch of woods up there. I couldn't get very close, but she stayed in the buggy. I had the idea she was waiting to meet someone who hadn't arrived yet."

"Nymon and Crunch."

"Probably. Did I spoil your supper?"

O'Grady chuckled. "Eckstrom, it might be good to have you around, after all. You draw me a map of exactly where you went. Soon as it gets dark, I'll ride up there and handle the rest of the Flint Nymon gang."

"No," Lacey Eckstrom said. "The only way you go up there and find the camp is if I show you where it is."

O'Grady looked at her as if she was crazy. "Damn female," he said softly.

"What was that, O'Grady?"

He took a deep breath and looked back at her. "I said damn right I want you along."

Lacey grinned, knowing better. "What I figured you said. Now, how about some dessert? The cherry pie is just like Mother used to make."

9

Lacey said she had ridden about seven miles north that afternoon when she was tracking the woman, so they began two hours before dark and moved up the same trail the lady agent had taken earlier.

Both had changed clothes. O'Grady wore blue jeans and a light-blue shirt with a leather vest and a broad-brimmed brown hat. He had the six-gun on his hip but no rifle. A long gun was for day use. At night he needed to be up close for identification.

Lacey wore a divided heavy blue skirt and sat a straight western saddle. She had on a light-blue blouse and a kerchief and a white western hat with a flat crown and a wide brim.

It got dark a half-mile before they came up to the thick woodsy section along a feeder stream that Lacey said must be the hideout.

"She parked the rig just inside that first screen of brush, but I could see it because I watched her drive in. She really could handle that horse and rig well."

"Notice anything new here right now?" he asked.

She looked, shook her head.

"We're slightly downwind of that place. Can you smell wood smoke?"

She sniffed the air and her nose quivered. "Yes. It's so fresh out here that smoke taint is easy to pick out, once I know what I'm smelling for."

"I'd say that means the men have arrived and the reunion is under way. They might plan on staying right here until the time for the debate. They've hit all the banks in the immediate area except the one in Ottawa. That would be a little too bold even for Nymon.

"Let's dismount and wait here for another hour, then I'll move up and see where they're camped and who is there. I might be able to finish this assignment right here."

"I'm coming along," Lacey said.

"No."

"Yes. If you want to keep me here, you'll have to tie me up, and if you try that, I'll fire my weapon and scare them away. I will, I swear."

"I knew this wasn't going to work out." He scowled in the darkness. "All right. You want to be an equal partner, you are. That means you take care of your own hide. I'm not going to be protecting you."

"Fine."

"Fine," he shot back. "You get in trouble, you get out of it yourself."

"Fine."

"Fine."

They stared at each other a moment in the moonlight.

"Hell, let's get moving now. It's dark enough." He moved out on foot across an open space toward the near edge of the heavily wooded area. When they arrived at the edge of the brush, he walked around the outside of it for fifty yards, then moved right into the brush for about twenty yards and stopped to listen. He heard laughter that seemed to come from directly ahead.

Canyon and Lacey worked forward slowly, carefully. They ducked under branches, or let them swing back silently. They didn't speak or even whisper. It was slow work.

Again they paused and listened. The sounds of voices and the crackle of a fire came faintly and now more to the right. They veered that way and soon could smell smoke again and hear the voices plainly.

"How much cash you get?" a woman's voice asked. The words came faintly but clear.

"Enough to buy you two more dresses. You must have about a hundred now."

"Not nearly enough. How much money?"

"About three thousand dollars."

"We're rich! Let's go to Chicago."

"You sure you didn't see anything suspicious in town?" the man's voice asked.

"There was this one man, about thirty. A redhead. I got the idea he was some kind of a politician."

"And you slept with him?"

"Best way to find out what a man is up to."

"You don't have to enjoy it so damn much."

O'Grady and Lacey worked forward again. Now they could see a fire winking through the brush.

As they moved up slowly, O'Grady wondered where Crunch was. He hadn't heard the other man say a word. The brush thinned now and they spotted the fire and two figures near it.

Lacey pushed up beside him, lying in the dirt and brush.

"We can't just shoot them down," Lacey whispered.

"Your suggestion?"

"Wait until morning and charge into them."

"Fine, and get one or both of us killed. These men are expert shots, marksmen, old West gunmen."

"Then your suggestion, O'Grady."

"Wait until they go to sleep. Slip up and tie them

tightly or knock them out and then tie them up, the two men.''

She considered it. "Best idea so far. They have rifles, so we can't chase them during the day. Yes, let's wait for them to go to sleep.''

"Problem. Where is the other man, Crunch?''

"On guard?''

"If so, he might find our horses.''

All of this had been whispered, and now they settled down to wait. Even with some sexy bouncing-around on the blankets, the outlaw pair should be sleeping soundly by midnight.

The talk at the fire quieted. For a minute O'Grady thought he saw a new shadowy form lift up near the fire, but he wasn't sure. After that they heard some movement, a few muffled words, and then silence.

The two agents lay there motionless for another hour. O'Grady used his body and the ground as a shield and lit a stinker match from a wax package. His watch showed that it was nearly midnight. He put out the match at once and stared at the fire, which now had burned down considerably.

He touched Lacey's shoulder and she lifted up. He drew his six-gun and motioned forward.

It was slow, agonizing work to move through the brush and leaf mulch on the ground without making a sound. They worked closer and closer, and at ten yards O'Grady lifted up and took a dozen quick steps forward. He turned and walked back out of the dim firelight faster than he went in. He touched her shoulder.

"Party's over,'' O'Grady said in his normal voice. "They left. While we were watching, they slipped out and left. I told you they were good.'' He was talking in a normal tone of voice now.

She stood. "How?''

"They might have found our horses. They sure

77

didn't see or hear us. I thought I saw a new form slip into the camp about an hour ago, and I must have been right. Did you see a saddle in the buggy the girl drove?"

"No."

"Probably was one there. All they had to do was unhitch the buggy, saddle the horse, and she could ride away with them. They must be ten miles from here by now. Nice try for us, but their side wins the battle."

"But not the war," Lacey said.

They made good time getting back to their horses. Both mounts were down. O'Grady swore and Lacey cried. The moonlight filtered through the light leaf cover on the two horses with their throats slashed. Both must have died within seconds and never had a chance to scream in terror.

"Hope you have your walking boots on," O'Grady said.

"We walking back to town?"

"Unless you can whip up a magical dragon to give us a ride."

"We could stay here until morning. We passed a small farm about two miles back."

He grinned at her in the moonlight. "And you don't mind sleeping out here with me tonight?"

"Not as long as you stay on your side of the creek."

"I think we better walk. Seven miles to town. We can do that in two hours. Most people can walk a mile in fifteen minutes." He paused. "Oh, I mean, most men can walk a mile in fifteen minutes. Maybe you can't."

"Can too!"

"Good. You prove it to me. Let's go."

A half-mile down the trail in the moonlight Lacey shook her head and glared at him. "You tricked me into walking back. I may never forgive you for that."

"Partners have to help each other. You just needed some convincing. Who better to convince you than your own pride."

"Don't remind me."

They passed the farmhouse later, but there were no lights on, so they walked on.

Twice they stopped to rest.

"Don't stop for me," Lacey said.

"Truce, Lacey. You've done much better than some men I've had to work with. That's why I like to work alone. Saints be praised, you've even been a help. So let's have a truce."

"I never did like war."

They shook hands, then continued their long hike back to town.

They didn't make it in two hours. With their stops it took them almost three hours. The room clerk was sleeping at his desk when they walked past him just after three A.M. The two agents both had rooms on the second floor; they went inside their respective rooms, locked doors, and fell into bed without undressing.

It had been a damn long day, O'Grady decided and went to sleep at once.

They both slept until nine and found each other in the dining room at nine-thirty.

"Do I look as bad as I feel?" Lacey asked him.

"You must feel terrible."

"Thanks, you're not God's gift to women yourself this morning."

"About the woman, Mary Jane or whatever her name is. Last night Crunch must have killed our horses, figured we were sneaking up on them and warned his boss and they all took off. But they don't know who was out there. So, if she does come back to town, maybe I can find out where their new camp is."

Lacey Eckstrom lifted her eyebrows in disbelief. "Yes, and maybe Marcella does know it was you out there last night and she'll wait her chance and kill you with her derringer. I bet she carries a .45 two-shot. Deadly."

"I'm touched that you're so concerned," O'Grady said, a tease in his voice.

"Concern isn't the right word, O'Grady. Without you to help on this case, I'll have to work twice as hard. Are we going in for some breakfast or just stand out here in the lobby and chat?"

They both ordered huge breakfasts and didn't say a word as they ate.

"If Marcella shows up in town again, I guess I'll just have to take the risk and talk to her. Now that I know who she is, I won't give her an opportunity to use that hideout. After we eat, let's go see the sheriff. Maybe your bottle of whiskey yielded more results last night with Pike than we got on our hike."

A half-hour later, Sheriff Tillery looked up from his desk as they walked in. He grinned. "By damn we got that one wrapped up." His bright-blue eyes sparkled. "Old Pike gave us three more names of people in on the plot to shoot Abe Lincoln. We've rounded them up. Problem is none of them will admit to knowing anything about it. A couple of them seemed downright surprised. 'Course we got no evidence to use against them. So I've told them all that we're going to be watching them close the next two weeks. Any misstep and wham! They're in jail. Old Pike's got a court date next week for attempted murder. Put an end to his blacksmithing."

"You think Pike gave you the right names?" Lacey asked.

The sheriff rubbed his fleshy face and frowned. "I truly hope so, Miss Eckstrom, I truly do. We got troubles enough without some more of my own people causing big problems.''

''Any messages for me on the telegraph wire from Washington?'' O'Grady asked.

''Not that I've seen,'' the sheriff said.

''I'd guess it's about time we talk with the two campaign managers,'' O'Grady said. He stood from the chair and looked at Lacey. ''You haven't met them yet, and we may have need of them before this is over. I'll be glad to introduce you.''

''Thanks.'' Lacey stood and weaved a moment from fatigue, then steadied and walked outside.

''We need to talk to the livery-stable man, too,'' Lacey said. ''How much is a horse like mine worth these days?''

''Fifty, maybe sixty dollars. We'll offer him forty for each one and he'll probably take it.''

They went to the livery first and the owner was in a mood to bargain. After a half-hour of haggling, they paid forty-five dollars for one of the horses and forty dollars for the other one.

''Was all that talk really necessary?'' Lacey asked, her eyes still heavy.

''Yes and no. Man wanted to bargain, I needed the practice. I figure we saved the government sixty-five dollars from the first price of seventy-five he wanted for each animal.''

He caught her arm and piloted her back down the street. They were almost to the door of the Plainsman Hotel before she looked up and realized where they were.

''What's going on here?''

''You're about ready to fall asleep on the march, so I figure I should walk you up to your door and be sure you sit down on your bed in your hotel room before you wind up snoozing away on the boardwalk somewhere like a common drunk."

"That won't . . ." A huge yawn stopped the words. She sagged against him as they started up the stairs. She straightened and looked at him with fire in her eyes. "You say one word . . ."

He held up both hands. "Hey, I've seen many a good man who couldn't stay up forty-eight hours in a row. No reflection on your womanliness or your ability to do this job like a man."

But he grinned as he opened her door and guided her to her bed. She sat down heavily, her eyelids sagging.

"You need any help from now on?" he asked with a straight face.

"No, thank you, Mr. O'Grady. I've no doubt that you're an expert at undressing women, but that's a job I can do for myself. Now, get out of here so I can have a nap. I'll see you for supper."

She slumped on the bed, waved feebly at him, and went to sleep.

O'Grady looked at her, smiled, then went to the door and slipped outside. He hurried down the hallway on his way to see the campaign managers.

10

O'Grady had put on his town clothes that morning even in his groggy state, and he now felt suitably dressed to call on a senator. He went up the steps to the headquarters of Stephen A. Douglas and knocked on the door.

It came open at once, manned by a volunteer from town, a pert, pretty young woman no more than twenty.

"Welcome to the headquarters of Stephen A. Douglas, senior senator from Illinois and the man who just might be the next president of the United States."

O'Grady smiled. "Quite a greeting, young lady. I'm here to see Mr. Alacron. Would you tell him that Canyon O'Grady is here? I'd appreciate it, darling."

The girl blushed and hurried to a door at the back of the small house's living room. A moment later Alacron came out and motioned for O'Grady to follow him through another door. It led into a downstairs bedroom.

Inside, he shook hands with O'Grady. "Yes, yes, glad you came over. I've been worried about those things happening to Abe. We don't want the Republicans to pull him out of the debate saying this part of Illinois is too pro-Douglas and Democratic."

"Mr. Alacron, I don't think that's a problem. My biggest worry right now is keeping Mr. Lincoln alive so he can be at the debate on the twenty-first."

"Yes, dreadful. I heard about the shooting. Just by luck I'd say that the dunderheads mistook that other man for Lincoln. It's a treatise on having your body-guards look as much like you as possible, I'd say. I'm going to have to change two of mine. Get short fat men more like the senator."

Both men laughed.

"I don't have anything important to tell you, Mr. Alacron. More to the point, I wondered if you have any ideas or suggestions for me. We've pretty well ruled out any large-scale show of force, such as an army company or some cavalry or even the local sheriff and deputies. What do you think?"

"Oh, I quite agree, I quite agree." Alacron wiped his brow with a linen handkerchief. O'Grady wondered if the man always sweat so much. Tall thin men wouldn't be prone to sweating, he didn't think. Again he was amazed how like a judge Randolph carried himself. "I really have no suggestions along those lines. I'd think you're right in keeping the troops out. Most of us in Illinois don't like the military to be too strong. Gunfire. Dreadful. Sometimes I think we should outlaw guns of all kinds except for the military and the lawmen. I know, I know, the constitution allows citizens the right to own and bear arms. Still, I can see many problems down through the years as we move from a rural society to a urban one like Chicago or Washington, D.C. Problems with firearms will multiply seriously."

"Yes, sir, you're probably right."

"But I'm glad you carry one, Mr. O'Grady. Then I don't have to." Both men chuckled again. "I know you don't vote in Illinois, Mr. O'Grady, but I wondered if you'd like to meet the senator. Remember this is the man who just probably will run for president two years from now. If he runs, he'll win. This might be your only chance to shake hands with a future president!''

"I'd be honored, Mr. Alacron. Then, too, I want to be absolutely certain of who he is the day of the debate.''

"Yes, good. Well-thought-out. Why don't you come this way? The senator is having lunch upstairs, but he should be finished by now.''

They went back into the living room, through a phalanx of volunteer workers, and up a closed stairway to the second floor. It had been converted into two big rooms, opening off the stairs. In one of them, Senator Stephen A. Douglas relaxed in a big chair with his feet on an ottoman and a long, brown cigar in his mouth.

"Senator, this is the federal security expert I was telling you about. The president sent him out when there were rumors of some danger to you at the debate.''

The senator put his feet down but didn't stand. He took out the cigar and looked over O'Grady. "Yes, I've seen you around town. You look big enough to handle most any trouble.'' He held out his hand. O'Grady stepped up and shook the senator's hand: it was soft and had little grip.

"It's a pleasure to meet you, Senator Douglas. I wish you all good fortune in the debate and the upcoming election. I hope Mr. Alacron has been telling you about our concern.''

"I . . . I didn't think the senator needed to know the details of the—'' Alacron began.

Senator Douglas quieted him with a stony stare. "Mr. O'Grady, just what's the president's concern again? I know we're of the same party, still that hardly seems cause to send a federal security agent all the way out here.''

"The Justice Department has intercepted some details about a plot to assassinate you or Mr. Lincoln, or perhaps both of you during the debate. Our sources say it's a matter of the slavery question. Some foreign powers are afraid that if you're elected senator, you'll go on to be president and surely a civil war will start that would ruin this foreign power's shipping industry.''

The senator stood and padded around the room in slippers. ''Fancy the same thing would happen if Abe beat me for the Senate seat and became president. He's far more radical on the slavery thing than I am.'' The senator turned and stared hard at O'Grady. ''Justice Department people take this threat seriously?'' Douglas asked.

''Oh, yes, indeed. We've already captured one of the party of the outlaw gang hired to do the job. There are two more of them and a woman. We're tracking her—and I saw, but couldn't capture or kill, the other two outlaws last night seven miles north of Ottawa. We take the threats with a great deal of seriousness.''

The senator turned to his campaign manager. ''Thanks for keeping me up to date, Randolph. You said we shouldn't be worried about this situation.''

''Actually, Senator, it might be better to keep things as nearly normal as possible so we don't tip off the outlaws we know of their mission. That way it will be easier for us to capture them.''

''Hasn't worked so far, has it?''

''No, Senator. Not yet. We still have ten days to the debate,'' Canyon said.

The senator's face cracked into a smile. ''Damn you young people. Supremely confident. I guess I was that way when I was in my late twenties. All right. Normal is the call. I'll vote for that. Well, good to talk to you. I have a meeting this afternoon, and I promised myself a short nap first.''

''Thank you, Senator. It's been good to meet you.

We'll keep you as safe as if you were in your Senate office.''

"Don't say that, O'Grady. Two senators got shot in their Washington offices last term."

O'Grady left the senator's headquarters not knowing whether to believe him or not about the two shootings. He had been pleased to meet the smallish man who could be the next president. He'd have a story to tell his grandchildren—if he ever had any children.

There was no banner outside Mr. Lincoln's campaign headquarters as there had been two days before. The shooting changed that. Now a guard at the door saw Canyon's weapon and held out his hand.

"New rule, no firearms inside the headquarters," the tough-looking young man said.

"I'm a federal agent here to protect Mr. Lincoln," O'Grady said.

"Sorry, no exceptions."

The two men stared at each other for a moment, then Onan Sanborn hurried up.

"It's all right in this case, Greg, he's a lawman," Sanborn said.

The guard stepped aside and Sanborn hurried O'Grady into a small room that had been turned into an office with desk and chairs.

"I hear the sheriff had to let those other three men go. Why did he do that?"

"They had no evidence against them, just a drunken spouting of names. But they have Pike. He'll go to prison for sure. How is Mr. Lincoln taking the whole thing?"

"Calmly. He says he's been shot at before, and by just as bad shots as those three were. He was in the upstairs bedroom at the time. Abe is not an early riser, except when I let him take his morning buggy drive.

He likes to wheel a team out the river road and back about daylight.''

"Not a good idea," O'Grady said.

"We know it—and he does, too. But he says he won't be a prisoner in a house or a town.''

"So, this is the second time someone has tried to kill Abe in Ottawa. Will there be a third one?''

"Probably. The man caught, Pike, is not much of a thinker. He wouldn't have the imagination to try this on his own. So there is an idea man, a mastermind, back there somewhere pulling the strings, and perhaps throwing the kerosene and pulling the trigger. Albeit a rather poor shot.''

"Goddamn!''

"I understand your concern. Do you have any suggestions what we could do to provide more protection during the debate? If it would only rain, we could move it into the biggest hall in town.''

"That would be the Catholic church. But it won't rain, and Abe won't agree to move inside anyway. I talked to him about it.'' Sanborn walked to the window and looked out. "A peaceful little town like this. How can it turn so vicious and deadly?''

"It's not only the town, Mr. Sanborn. Nymon and his man are two ugly, vicious killers who will do anything for money. Yesterday they shot down two men in a bank five miles east of town. They are animals.''

Sanborn shuddered. "Somehow we have to protect Lincoln. He is going to be a great man someday. Have you ever met him?''

O'Grady shook his head.

"Come, I'm sure he'll have time to see you. He's quite a remarkable man. Remarkable.''

They went through the office, which was much like that in Douglas' house. Upstairs at the front of the building, a small bedroom held a brass bed and a heavy mattress with a simple hand-stitched quilt thrown over it.

The man who sat in the straight-backed wooden chair was sparse and thin, and his long legs stuck out heading two different directions. He wore a simple black suit and white shirt but no necktie. As soon as Sanborn came into the room, he stood and turned. His face was craggy, eyes deep set, high cheekbones with hollows below them, and a square chin. He wore no beard or mustache.

"Onan, I had a thought . . ." Abraham Lincoln stopped as he noticed the guest.

"Mr. Lincoln, this is the federal agent in town to keep an eye on us. Canyon O'Grady, I'd like you to meet the next senator from the great state of Illinois, Abraham Lincoln. Mr. Lincoln, this is Canyon O'Grady."

The politician pushed out his bony hand and O'Grady shook it. The hand was warm and strong, and O'Grady knew there were calluses on the fingers.

"A pleasure to meet you, Mr. Lincoln," O'Grady said.

"Young man, it's good to meet you. Now, I don't want you to fret about that little scuffle at the front door. Harvey is going to be just fine, so no great damage done."

"It could get worse, Mr. Lincoln, but I hope not. Has Mr. Sanborn told you about my job here and the Justice Department's report?"

"Yes, all of it. I also received a letter from the Justice people. Very kind of them, and of you. This is just a little old state election out here in the wilds of Illinois."

O'Grady liked this rawboned, rough-cut man at once. He smiled. "Mr. Lincoln, I hear that you're one of the top contenders for the Republican nomination for president. These debates must be vitally important to you.''

The man born in a log cabin smiled. ''So people say. Just hope you don't call off the debate or push us inside. A politician has to get a feel of the people. I do that best out in the sunshine and with a nice little breeze blowing.''

''We hope to have the outlaws well in hand before the debate date, Mr. Lincoln. Oh, if you get an urge to go for a drive early in the morning, take along a bodyguard, or give me a whistle and I'll go with you. A trip like that from now on could be on the dangerous side.''

The tall man smiled down at O'Grady, who felt short in this man's presence. He almost laughed, then nodded. ''I just might do that. Bet you can use that revolver. I used to do a bit of hunting with a muzzle-loader rifle.'' His face softened and O'Grady felt the man had transported himself back twenty years to his early, happy days.

''Mr. Lincoln, I better be going. It's been a real pleasure to meet you. Try not to think about this threat. That's my work. Good luck on the debates.''

They shook hands again and O'Grady felt a tingle go up his arm. This tall man exuded an aura, a power, a confidence that seemed to be catching. What a contrast between this man and Senator Douglas.

O'Grady went out the front door and turned and looked back. A small house in a small town in the middle of Illinois. He hoped the political career of that man of the people didn't end here with an assassin's bullet.

Dammit, he had to make sure that it didn't . . . which meant he had to dig out Nymon and his last gang member quickly.

11

Kirk closed up his hardware store. It was after six-thirty and quitting time. He blew out the only lantern he had lit, and went to the back of the building. Instead of leaving as he usually did, Kirk went to the basement door, opened it, and went down the dimly lit steps. A coal-oil lamp glowed on a table below where Barnaby sat. He looked up and disgustedly threw down a pencil on a pad of paper. He watched Kirk and swore.

"By damn, Kirk, I hope you have some good ideas. I haven't come up with much. The only good thing that's happened for us so far is that Pike didn't give our names to the sheriff as the other two who shot at Lincoln. Pike must have been so drunk he forgot who we were."

Kirk sat on a chair across from his partner in this attempt to kill Abe Lincoln, and put two bottles of warm beer on the table. Barnaby grabbed one of them.

"Why do you always think I'm dumb, Barnaby? I got lots of good ideas. You always think that because you're a back-country lawyer, you're the brains around here."

"So you've got some good ideas, Kirk. Come on, give me one right now."

"Don't mind if I do. I been thinking on it most of the day. You see, this Lincoln guy likes to go on morning drives, early, about five A.M. He drives a one-horse rig and he goes alone."

Barnaby sat up suddenly. He had been pulling at the warm beer. Now he put the bottle on the table, his eyes widened, and he grinned. "No shit?"

"Absolutely. When he's going the next morning, he has the livery man leave the rig behind his house with a horse harnessed in it and ready to go. All we have to do is check tonight about midnight and see if the rig is there. If it is, he's probably going tomorrow morning."

"And if it is, we trail him out of town tomorrow at five A.M., stop him at gunpoint, and then arrange an absolutely terrible and fatal buggy accident for him," Barnaby continued. "It sounds perfect."

"Last three mornings, he's gone out the river road. Done the driving by himself, and not even another buggy goes with him. Sounds just about damn perfect to me, smart-assed lawyer man."

"Kirk, you're a marvel. I don't even want to know how you found out. I'll check the house tonight. Will the rig be in front of the house or in the alley behind the place?"

"Behind it. What will we do once we get him out there on the river road alone?"

"Mr. Lincoln will have a terrible accident. His rig will crash, maybe even into the river. A tragic, fatal accident. We'll see that it's an accident that no one can question. A runaway horse probably. But there'll be no witnesses."

"No guns?" Kirk asked.

"Kirk, it's hard to make it look like an accident if the man has a couple of bullet holes in him. Right? Clubs will make it seem more like a real wreck. If the rig is there, I'll stop by and tell you tonight."

"You have a horse?" Kirk asked.

Barnaby snapped his fingers. "Damn, I better get down to the livery tonight and rent one just in case. I know you have one in that little shed of yours. You have two?''

Kirk shook his head.

Later that night, Barnaby stopped at Kirk's house and reported that the one-horse rig was harnessed up and waiting behind Lincoln's rented place.

"See you a block down from the Lincoln house at four-thirty in the morning," Barnaby said, excitement spilling into his voice. "We'll stay out of sight until we're sure he's going out the river road.

"I'll bring a revolver to use to get him to stop the rig. Then we'll find the right place for the accident.''

The next morning, the two conspirators sat on their horses in the alley on the other side of Lincoln's rented house and watched the black buggy. At a quarter to five, they saw three men come out of the Lincoln house. They talked a moment, seemed to argue, then the tallest in the group shook his head under the black hat he wore and stepped into the buggy and drove away down the alley the other way.

Barnaby grinned. "Looks like today is the one we've been waiting for.'' They rode out and paralleled the buggy as it came to the next street, went up half a block and then south toward the stream on the river road.

Kirk and Barnaby let the rig stay a quarter-mile ahead until it was three miles out of town, then they put on a spurt of speed and galloped forward until they caught up to it. It did not speed up. Now for the first time they saw that the one-horse rig had side curtains, making it hard for them to see who was inside.

Barnaby spurred his mount ahead of the trotting buggy horse and waved his six-gun at the driver. It had no effect on the driver; the rig didn't slow down. Barnaby swore, cocked the weapon, and fired a shot in front of the horse, then cocked it again and aimed at the driver.

"Stop! Stop the buggy," Barnaby bellowed.

This time the horse began to slow and came to a gradual stop. The two men rode up on each side of the buggy and waited. No one came out of it.

"Step down now, or I'll shoot your horse," Barnaby roared.

There was no movement from the rig. Barnaby stepped his horse closer to the black curtain and suddenly the reins slapped against the horse's back and the buggy jolted forward, racing down the river road at a gallop.

"Damn, damn," Barnaby shouted, and pulled his mount around to give chase. This time it took him considerable time to catch up with the buggy, and as he did, he sent a shot through the back of the canvas top. It had no effect on the speed of the buggy.

Barnaby raced alongside the closed rig, trying to jerk off the side curtain, but the offset wheels kept him too far away. At last he surged ahead, grabbed the horse's bridle, and slowed it down with his own mount.

When the horse had come to a stop, he looked inside the dusky interior of the buggy.

"Step down, damn you," Barnaby thundered. "We've had enough of this running away."

"I quite agree," Canyon O'Grady said, jumping down from the buggy on the same side where Barnaby sat his horse. O'Grady's six-gun was out and covering Barnaby, who had put his weapon back in its holster when he grabbed the buggy horse's bridle.

"What the hell? You're not Abe Lincoln," Barnaby blurted.

"And you're not President Buchanan," O'Grady said. He looked around for the other rider, but he had pulled up when the rig stopped and hung back out of pistol range. When he saw the driver wasn't Lincoln, Kirk turned and rode fast back for town.

O'Grady walked up and lifted the six-gun out of Barnaby's holster. "Get down from there," O'Grady said.

"Why? Who are you?"

"Why get down? Because if you don't, I'll shoot you off the horse. Good enough? Who am I? I'm the guy who's going to shoot you off the horse if you don't get down."

Barnaby slid off the horse on O'Grady's side. He pretended to turn his ankle and cried out in pain and bent to rub his ankle. When he came up, he had a hideout derringer that spat out a .45 round.

O'Grady saw the derringer clear the boot top and fired just before Barnaby did. O'Grady's round smashed through the lawyer's upper chest, nicked his left lung, and lodged somewhere near his spine. He slammed backward against his horse and then slid to the ground. His own derringer round dug into the ground at his feet and the small weapon spilled out of his hand as the bullet jolted into him.

O'Grady was at his side at once, kneeling in the sand. "Who was the man with you?" Canyon demanded.

Barnaby's eyes flickered open. "Who? President Buchanan," he said, then passed out.

O'Grady checked him. He wasn't dead. He loaded the man into the buggy seat and headed back toward town.

Who were these people? He'd have an interesting session questioning this man when he got him back to town and to the doctor's office. If he was local, the sheriff would know him.

Now he was thankful that Onan Sanborn had sent him a note last night about Mr. Lincoln's insistence on taking his morning drive again today. O'Grady had arrived at the Lincoln house at four A.M. and he and Sanborn had discussed the situation with Lincoln for almost an hour.

At last Sanborn had prevailed. Lincoln had grudgingly let O'Grady take his place, but said he was sure they were being overprotective.

After this early-morning close call, O'Grady was sure that Mr. Lincoln would listen to his advisers a little more. Lincoln would realize that he couldn't do the state of Illinois any good at all if he was filling up a cemetery plot somewhere.

Back at the sheriff's office, a deputy ran for the doctor and O'Grady wrote out charges against Barnaby: attempted murder, assault and battery, and attempted robbery of a vehicle on a public roadway. Still unconscious when the doctor finished with him, Barnaby was put in a cell, and O'Grady assured the deputy in charge he would be back to question the man.

Outside the sheriff's office, Lacey came riding up and talked to O'Grady. "Deputy Carson and I watched the river road starting at five A.M. as you suggested," she said. "We saw you drive out in the buggy and two men follow you, but the deputy couldn't identify either one. Then maybe forty-five minutes later, we saw one man galloping fast back into town. This time Deputy Carson rode out as if heading out the road. When he came back, he said he got a good look at the man. He's Kirk Danzing. Owns the Ottawa Hardware Store."

"Good work. We know who the other one is, but we don't have enough evidence on this Kirk for a court of law. We'll watch him, though. I want you to do that. Park yourself somewhere around the hardware store, take a book to read, and a notebook. I want to know where Kirk goes before the store opens. Where he has lunch, what he does after the store closes. Damn important."

"Starting now."

"Starting a half-hour ago."

"Will I get to meet Senator Douglas and Mr. Lincoln?" Lacey asked.

"Yes, but later."

"Fine." She turned and rode away toward the store.

O'Grady went around to the back and drove the black buggy down to the alley behind the rented Lincoln house. Sanborn swore for five minutes when he saw the bullet hole in the buggy top and heard the story.

Abe Lincoln lifted shaggy brows and nodded. "I was wrong. Been known to happen before. No more morning drives. I'll even stay indoors if that will make everyone happy. Want to study up on a couple of state issues anyway." The candidate went back inside the house.

"So there are two groups trying to kill the candidates," Sanborn said, his face tight, eyes half-closed in anger.

"We've got at least two of the locals. Know about another one we're watching. I'm more concerned where Nymon's Raiders are and what they're up to. The two of them left are more dangerous than a dozen of these local amateurs."

"So what can we do about Nymon?" Sanborn asked.

"Not a hell of a lot until they show themselves or we get another whiff of where they are. How are the preparations for the debate coming along?"

"We've worked out some of the guidelines. But I'm afraid once these two get started, it's going to be a free-for-all. Both men have strong opinions."

"Let's just hope that we can keep both men alive till the debate," O'Grady said. He left the rig there and walked down Main Street watching for Lacey. She wore a blue dress today and a little blue hat. Not the best outfit for a shadow job.

He found her in the general store near the front window, watching the Ottawa Hardware Store across the street.

"He's inside and hasn't been out so far this morning, at least out the front. I can't very well watch both front and back doors."

"I'll be back to spell you so you can get some dinner this noon," O'Grady said. "Right now I need to talk to Douglas' manager. He might have heard something, might have some ideas."

She looked up and started to say something, then stopped.

"Go ahead, say it, Lacey. Whatever it is, I'm not going to get mad, and if it concerns the investigation, it might help."

"No, it won't help the investigation. About you going in Lincoln's buggy this morning. You could have been shot and killed out there."

"Yeah. Told you it wasn't all glamour and high living out here in the field for us agents. But you wouldn't believe me."

"I will now. Where . . . where were you when the man shot through the back of the buggy?"

"Crouched down on the bottom of the floorboards as low as I could get. I was behind the padded back and the wooden seat. It would have taken a rifle round to get through all that protection." He grinned at her expression. "Sometimes smart is better than brave. Remember that. Don't do anything dumb trying to get some information, or capture a suspect."

Her look of awe had tempered to one of mild approval and at last she grinned. "Okay, I'm back to normal again. Get out of here before Kirk spots us together and figures out we're on the same team. Did he identify you this morning?"

"Doubt it, he was thirty, forty yards away when I

shot Barnaby. But you're right. I'll sit out in the sunshine when I come back to relieve you." He walked out of the store and down the street to Senator Douglas' campaign headquarters. There was red-white-and-blue bunting on the door and below the windows. A large drawing of the senator perched over the door.

O'Grady walked in and asked to see Mr. Alacron.

There was a different pretty girl than the one he saw the last time. She said Mr. Alacron was busy.

"Please tell him that O'Grady is here and needs to talk to him as soon as possible." He put on his best smile and saw her react. "Tell him it really is important. I think he'll want to see me."

She nodded, smiled, and walked away. A minute later she was back her smile wider now. "He said you should go right in. You must be an important person; he hasn't seen *anybody* all morning."

She left the door open to let him in, and as he brushed past her to get inside, he gently touched her shoulder with his arm. She smiled again and closed the door.

"Mr. O'Grady," Randolph said with a touch of panic. "Damn glad that you stopped by. I was about ready to go out and try to find you. I just found a threatening letter in my morning stack of mail. Look at this damn thing!"

He held out a piece of paper. A delicate feminine hand had written:

> Mr. Alacron,
> Don't work too hard for Senator Douglas. By August 21st he's going to be dead. Nothing you can do can possibly stop it.
>
> Flint Nymon.

12

Randolph Alacron glared at the piece of paper and then up at Canyon O'Grady. "Have you ever seen such nerve, such audacity, such outlandishness! Can he do what he claims he can do, O'Grady?"

O'Grady handed him back the piece of paper. "Mr. Alacron, since the time of Julius Caesar, ambitious men have been assassinating political leaders. Nowadays if a man wants to kill another—and is willing to sacrifice his life to accomplish that task—there is absolutely no way to give the target one-hundred-percent protection.

"If old Julius had stayed at home from the Roman senate that day on the fifteenth of March, he would have lived a lot longer. Who can say what might happen here?

"I can tell you this about Flint Nymon: he's a violent man capable of anything. But he's human; he can die. And his demise is what it's going to take to stop him from killing someone here in Ottawa on the twenty-first of August.

"My job is to find him and stop him." O'Grady looked around the room. "Who else has seen this letter?"

"No one, not even the senator."

"Give it to me and don't tell anyone about this. One thing we don't need is panic by the faithful. I just hope that Nymon didn't send the same message to the local newspaper."

"The editor is a friend of mine," Alacron said. "He wouldn't print anything like this without talking to me about it."

"Good. Did you know there was another attempt on Mr. Lincoln's life this morning? It failed, and we caught another local. I can't figure out their motivation. I suggest you limit the senator's movements as much as possible. No public meetings before the debate. No speaking engagements, no crowds. Keep him indoors as much as possible."

"That won't be overly hard. The senator is not an outdoor enthusiast as is Mr. Lincoln."

"Good. Now don't worry about this letter. Be concerned, but don't worry. Worry is my job."

"You say there was an attempt on Mr. Lincoln's life this morning?"

O'Grady told him briefly about the encounter, and added that one of the men had been captured but the other one escaped.

"Local men, you said?"

"Yes, the one we captured is called Barnaby, an Ottawa lawyer."

"Barnaby . . . Barnaby . . . I've met some of the locals but that name doesn't register. Who was the other one?"

"Still working on that." O'Grady decided not to mention Kirk. "Remember, not a word about this to anyone." He picked up his hat and walked out of the headquarters.

On the street again, Canyon checked his pocket watch. He still had nearly two hours to midday. It made for a long morning when you got up at three in the morning.

He walked out to the Willoughby Inn to talk to the

manager. The man, in his sixties, had run the inn for over thirty years and was proud of the old place.

Quickly, O'Grady told the man, Amos Gunderslaugh, who he was and why he was in town.

"I don't expect that this killer gang will stay at your inn, Mr. Gunderslaugh. But they are supposed to be meeting someone here. Do you have any foreigners here, an Englishman by any chance?"

"We most certainly do. Two," the innkeeper said. "Both are schoolteachers, I believe. Miss Emily is about forty, and Miss Elizabeth is about thirty-five. Both very proper. I even take tea to them in the afternoon."

"Two women. No men?"

Gunderslaugh shook his head.

"No men from Germany or France, or even Spain?" Canyon asked.

"I'm afraid not."

"I'm at the Plainsman. If you get one or two Englishmen or other foreign men in here in the next week, be sure to send me a sealed note to my room at the Plainsman. I'll be grateful, and so will the president of the United States."

"You've seen him?" Gunderslaugh asked.

"Yes, a week ago. He gave me this assignment in his office in the White House."

"Glory be! Wait until I tell Martha."

"You will send me a sealed note if men like that register?"

"Oh, yes indeed! It will be my pleasure. Deliver it myself, Mr. O'Grady."

It was eleven by the time he got back to the center of town, so he had an early dinner. He changed his mind and had breakfast instead, a stack of wheat cakes, six strips of thick bacon, four sausage patties, three eggs, and four slices of toast around half a gallon of black, hot coffee. He wouldn't be hungry again until three o'clock.

Canyon walked into the hardware store and bought a small box of .45 rounds. The short man, Mr. Kirk Danzing himself, waited on O'Grady. He took no special notice, nor did he even look up when he got paid. The man seemed to have his mind on something else.

Outside, O'Grady stretched and looked over at the general store, then walked across the wide dirt street and sat in one of the chairs in front of the store. He tilted the chair back against the wall and pulled his hat down to keep the sun out of his eyes and so it covered most of his face. He closed his eyes for just a moment, but snapped them open. A man with only three hours' sleep the night before could go to sleep in a thrice this way.

A woman in a blue dress came down the steps and walked past him, then changed her mind and went the other way and slipped into Delmonico's Restaurant.

O'Grady sat and watched the hardware store across the street. He hated this part, waiting and watching. But he had become an expert at it. He had learned to lie Indian-still for three hours straight if he had to, never moving an arm or a leg. Patience was the only way to stay alive sometimes.

A half-hour later, Kirk came out of his store and looked down the street, then went back in. That night, O'Grady decided, he would watch the back door and let Lacey stake out the front one.

Damn, he wished he could take just a ten-minute nap. His eyes closed and he snapped them open. A nap now would last until Lacey came back and kicked him in the shins.

Another uneventful half-hour passed and then Lacey came back. She slowed as she passed in front of him. No one else was near.

"You keep on the front," Canyon said. "I'll go into the alley and watch the back. When he closes up, come around and find me."

She never missed a step but nodded and walked on down to a dress shop, where she would have another good view of the hardware store.

O'Grady stood, stretched, and reset his hat, then walked unhurriedly down the street and turned on the cross street to find the alley that ran behind the hardware store. The alley was twenty feet wide, with more stores and a few houses backed up to it on the next street. He found Ottawa Hardware by counting in from the corner, then he saw a small sign that identified the back door for customers. There was a small dock where rolls of wire and pipe and other heavy items had been stacked in wooden racks.

O'Grady found a door across the alley where several large empty cardboard containers had been piled. He pulled two of them together and left a slot between them. Now he could sit behind the boxes with his back to the building and see the whole dock and back door of Ottawa Hardware.

He waited.

A pair of flies tried to drive him crazy. He caught one in his hand after three tries, but the other one darted away. He'd heard once that most flies lived only seven to nine days. How did they get so smart and become such good flyers so quickly? Still, if your whole life was seven days long, you had to get a fast start.

A farm wagon rolled up the alley and a man in overalls backed it up to the dock. He went into the hardware store, and a short time later, Kirk came out with the farmer, unlocked a chain through a row of rolls of smooth wire, and carried six of them to the wagon.

They went back inside and a few minutes later the farmer came out and drove away.

O'Grady had plenty of time to think. The letter from Nymon bothered him, but did not generate any panic. The man was a complete egotist, so damn sure of himself that he could warn one of his potential victims.

He checked his watch. One-thirty.

A horse and buggy clattered down the alley and woke up O'Grady. He realized he'd been sleeping. Damn! What had he missed? He scowled and rubbed his face with his hands. He had probably missed nothing. What could Kirk do in broad daylight? He would wait until tonight. After dark, that was more Kirk's style.

He looked at his watch. It was past four-thirty. He had slept for three hours. O'Grady slipped out from behind the boxes and walked the length of the alley and came back. He checked to be sure no one was watching, then slid in behind the boxes again.

When it got dark, he would move closer to the hardware store. He had picked out a spot on the dock, ten feet from the door but behind a stack of cedar fence posts.

For now he waited.

Three more wagons went through the alley.

One leghorn hen and ten chicks wandered along clucking and cheeping, hunting for some dropped oats or wheat.

A boy in his teens wandered into the alley, looked down the length, and then motioned. A girl about the same age hurried in and they both leaned against the wall three stores along. They must be sure no one could see them. They talked softly and she smiled. She was maybe sixteen, pretty, with long brown hair. The boy reached over and, without touching her otherwise, kissed her lips. The kiss ended and he pushed against her and kissed her again, this time his hand covering one of her breasts. She laughed and shook her head and ran back to the street. The boy grinned and followed her.

O'Grady grinned, too. The boy knew there was another alley just down the street.

By six o'clock that night he saw the town's life slowing. Three store owners had come out and closed back doors and shutters on windows.

A little later Kirk came out and checked his chains and put locks on them around merchandise, then he went inside and closed the back door.

Slowly the summer sun sank in the sky and it was dusk. Just before full dark, a tall man came down the alley with a solid, firm stride, as if he knew where he was going. He angled in at Ottawa Hardware and turned the knob on the small door. It came open and he vanished inside.

A visitor. An after-dark visitor. Perhaps a collaborator-visitor. A tall thin man. Sure, O'Grady thought. There probably were thirty or forty such men in town.

A short time later another figure came into the alley mouth and walked forward. This one was tentative, obviously counting the backs of stores. When the figure came closer, O'Grady could see the dress and small hat. Lacey.

"Over here," he whispered, and she turned and walked toward the boxes. He pulled her down beside him.

"Miss Eckstrom, I presume? Crack U.S. field agent who is absolutely fearless and ready to tackle any problem, anywhere?"

She turned and looked at him in the pale light coming from a half-moon. "Don't tease me, O'Grady. Right now I'm still scared pink. I've never walked down a dark alley before expecting to be assaulted and murdered at any minute. I was just ready to come in to this alley when that man beat me to it. Where did he go?''

''You're the detective. You tell me where.''

She scowled and shook her head. ''Look, I'm sorry for some of those things I said that first night. I was even more scared then than I am now. I thought you might explode and embarrass me and send me back to Washington. So I struck out. Now have a little pity on a defenseless, unskilled mere woman.''

He touched her shoulder and she didn't pull away. ''Okay, sorry. No more teasing. The man went into Kirk's hardware store. Did you get a good look at him?''

''No, tall and thin wearing mostly black. Nothing more.''

''About all I could see. He went in like he was expected.''

''Should we charge in there and arrest them?''

''No charges, no evidence.'' He paused. ''Look, this could take half the night. You didn't get much sleep last night. Why don't you get back to your room and get some sleep.''

''I have a better idea,'' Lacey said. ''Anyway, I must admit I dozed off for a couple of hours this afternoon. Why don't you take a nap and I'll keep watch. If anything happens, I'll wake you and we'll both be here.''

O'Grady grinned. ''So this time you don't mind sleeping with me. We're making progress.''

She laughed softly. ''The man-animal again. O'Grady, I'm not sleeping with you. You're having a nap near me. That's all. That is, unless you had a longer nap this afternoon than I did.''

''You win. I could use some sleep. If anyone comes out, or goes in, you promise to wake me.''

"Promise. Now go to sleep."

She had sat down beside him when she first arrived. They both had their backs against the building. Now he closed his eyes, crossed his arms, and began to breathe deeply. Slowly his head leaned toward her. Then it settled on her shoulder and he moved slightly and sighed.

"You better be sleeping, Canyon O'Grady," she whispered. She waited a minute and then grinned.

O'Grady waited for more response, then opened one eye. She couldn't see his face. He grinned, then slowly closed his eyes. It was a nice soft, beautiful little shoulder, he decided. Before he got any further with his small interesting fantasy, he drifted off to sleep.

Lacey Eckstrom sat there with Canyon's head on her shoulder and watched the alley and the hardware store's back door. She glanced down at him and grinned. He might not be such a bear to work with, after all. So far, so good.

He moved and one of his arms fell from their crossed position and ended in her lap. She let it lay there a moment, then lifted it gently and moved it back on his legs. He never noticed.

A half-hour later a buggy clattered through the alley, the one horse snorting, but it kept going past the hardware store. O'Grady was awake with the first jangle of the harness. He lifted his head from her shoulder and watched the rig.

"Going past," she whispered, and he nodded. She guided his head back to her shoulder. It rested there a moment, then fell forward, barely grazed one breast, and a few seconds later his head lay in her lap.

She moved slightly, her frown fully in place. "O'Grady," she whispered. "O'Grady," she said louder right in his ear.

He stirred and one hand came up and rested under his head and on her upper thigh.

"Oh, damn," Lacey said and let him lay where he was.

O'Grady lay there with a sly grin on his face and both eyes wide open. He knew she couldn't see him. Yes, he was making progress with this new detective-type agent, he decided. Then his eyes closed and he slept.

It was almost an hour later when she shook his shoulder; he came awake quietly, fully alert at once, knowing exactly where he was and what the situation was. He lifted up from her lap and saw two men come out from the darkened door of Kirk's store. One was short, Kirk; the other one was nearly a foot taller. O'Grady couldn't make out any features or distinguishing clothing or gear. The men talked a moment in whispers, then came to the alley and went in opposite directions.

When the tall man was halfway down the long stretch of alley, the two agents lifted up and silently followed him. They still might have a chance to find out who he was.

13

The man walking up the alley toward the rear of Ottawa Hardware did not look behind. He had no sense that anyone was watching him. He marched to the rear dock, up the three steps, and to the door. It was unlocked, as Kirk said it would be.

Inside, he found it totally dark. Then a door opened and he saw Kirk, who came quickly with a small lamp and locked the rear door, then led him down to the basement, where a table was set with pads of paper and bottles of beer and a large dish of freshly popped popcorn.

Kirk sat down and tipped his bottle of beer. He looked across the table at his visitor and let a frown play across his square-cut face.

"Mr. Alacron, what are we going to do about Pike and Barnaby?"

"We're going to do nothing, absolutely nothing. Pike has been a lost cause all along and Barnaby is smart enough to know not to talk about us. Don't worry about them. What we have to do is come up with a final and permanent way to get rid of Lincoln before the debate is set to start."

"How?" Kirk asked. "I've used up all the ideas that I had. I'm not sure what to do now."

"I have an idea. Do you know of anyone here who can cook up a batch of nitroglycerin?"

"Nitro? I've heard of that. Damn bad explosive. Powerful but unstable. Bump it and it could explode. About anybody around here doing it up? I don't think so. I sell black powder for stump- and rock-blasting, things like that, but nobody even asks about nitro."

"You have some black powder here in the store?"

"You're sitting about six feet from four kegs. Just got it in last week. Several men are clearing some land down by the river."

"So, of course, you have burning fuse to set off the charge?"

"Yeah, plenty . . . Shit! You thinking of setting off a blast to do in old Abe?"

"About the best thing we have left. He hasn't been seen outside his house the whole day. I'd bet he's been told to stay indoors. That federal agent told me to keep Douglas inside."

"How much powder? How big a charge you want to use?" Kirk asked.

"Depends where we put it and how close we can get it to Lincoln, wouldn't you think?" Alacron stood and paced back and forth.

Kirk looked up. "Barnaby never did say why you was so set on doing in Lincoln. Not many people outside the state ever heard of him."

"Oh but they have. He gave over fifty speeches three years ago trying to elect a Republican president. But he didn't succeed. If these debates go through, he just might get lucky and whip Senator Douglas. That would ruin the senator's plans for running for president two years hence.

"Nothing, not one damn thing, is going to interfere with the senator getting elected president of these United States. Those who help us will be remembered. There are a lot of jobs in Washington the new president will need to fill. Senator Douglas always remembers his friends.''

Randolph Alacron stopped pacing. He looked at the merchant. ''Now, Mr. Kirk Danzing, let's get busy and look at this black powder and figure out how much we can use, how much we can hide, where it can go, and when we want to detonate it. Tonight maybe?''

Kirk moved the table and opened a trapdoor in the wooden floor. A pit had been dug and in it were stacked four wooden kegs filled with black powder. They were oak and each weighed fifty pounds. It was enough blasting powder to level the whole hardware store and a few more besides.

One of the kegs had been opened. It had a large cork in the top where the powder could be poured out and weighed. They tugged the opened keg up to the floor and poured out what Kirk said was about five pounds of black powder.

''That's enough to blow down a barn,'' Kirk said. ''Put that under some of the center beams and it would shatter the sides of the barn outward and blow the whole damn thing into kindling.''

''How much to do the same thing to the house where Lincoln is staying? How about five pounds on each side and the fuses the same lengths so they would go off at the same time?''

''More than enough. Only trouble is, I couldn't never make them go off at the same instant. Damn fuse burns faster and slower, sometimes within inches. Can't tell. We had a farmer get his leg blowed off 'cause the fuse burned three feet in a split second. Sssssssst . . . boom! Should burn a foot a minute, but sometimes you can't tell.''

''One bomb, then. Lincoln sleeps upstairs in the front of the house. We can put the bomb at the side near the front and light it about three in the morning.

Nobody around then. Doubt if they have any guards outside. We'll blow him into a splinter and he won't ever wake up the next morning.''

Kirk sat back and looked at this dignified man talking so wild. "Barnaby said you was a little on the bloodthirsty side. I guess he was right."

"We protect our senator any way we can. What do we put that powder in? How about making it seven pounds so we're sure it'll do a good job?''

They put the black powder in a two-gallon painter's can that Kirk got from upstairs. They punched a hole in it midway and pushed in a two-foot length of burning fuse.

"You sure this will work?'' Alacron asked.

"Mr. Alacron, I blasted stumps for a living for two years. Yes, sir, it'll work."

"Want to do it tonight?'' Alacron asked.

"Tonight? Well, I don't know.'' Kirk shrugged. "Now to think on it, guess there's no reason why not. We got it all ready. What time?''

"Say we meet back here at two A.M. and make sure it's all right. Then we can check out the Lincoln place, set the little present in place, and light the fuse. Next we saunter away and then run like hell!''

They both laughed and then finished their beers.

"Guess that does it. I'll put the top on this paint can so it'll have more of a bang when it goes off. If we had a old stump to sit on this side of it, more of the blast would go into the house. Maybe we can dig it down a mite and get it under the floorboards. I think that house is built on pier blocks.''

"We'll check that out for sure about two this morning,'' Alacron said.

They went up the stairs and to the back door. There, Kirk blew out the small kerosene lamp he carried and put it on the floor, then they slipped out the back door.

113

They talked there for a minute, then Kirk locked the door and they went out the alley in the opposite directions.

Randolph Alacron strode through the soft evening toward the senator's headquarters. He was feeling better than he had in days. Now, at last they had a good solid chance to get rid of Lincoln.

He jumped up the steps to the Douglas campaign headquarters house two at a time and greeted the sweet young girl at the door.

"Mr. Alacron, there are several notes for you on your desk, and the senator wants to see you. He said as soon as you get in. He sounded upset about something."

Alacron stood close to her so no one else could see and patted her saucy little behind. "Thank you, Thelma," he said.

She grinned. "Thank you, Mr. Alacron."

He hurried into the senator's upstairs room.

"Where the hell have you been, Randolph?"

Alacron took off his hat and set it precisely on the dresser and nodded. "Mr. President, I've been working on your coming election. Can't start too soon on something like that."

"What's this I hear about Lincoln getting shot at this morning out on the river road?"

"True, a pair of robbers, evidently. They caught one and the other one got away. But it wasn't really Lincoln. A bodyguard or somebody rode in the rig instead."

"It wasn't a bodyguard, it was O'Grady, that government agent. Wonder how they got wind of something like that?"

"I'm sure I don't know. Now, what can I get for you? Anything you need? Would you like to have a back rub? I'm sure that sweet little Thelma downstairs would be thrilled to rub your back, and most anything else you wanted her to.''

''No, Randolph. I don't go in for that sort of thing. I've told you before. I'm looking forward to a nice long night's sleep. I just wanted to be sure about that Lincoln thing. Lock that downstairs door for me so nobody busts up here and ruins my sleep. See you in the morning, Al.''

Alacron went down the steps at once. He hated to be called Al. But then, the president of the United States could call him anything he wanted. For just a second he wondered what post he would ask for. Attorney general might be nice, or maybe the secretary of the treasury, or of war. He'd decide later.

He went downstairs and asked Thelma if she could help him in his office, which was also his bedroom. She smiled when she saw the big bed. He closed the door and nodded. ''Thelma, what I'm about to tell you is in the strictest of confidence. Agreed?''

''Oh, yes, Mr. Alacron.''

He stepped closer. ''Thelma, you've got the best-looking breasts I've ever seen.'' She looked up, surprised. He kissed her and fondled her breasts. When the kiss ended, she laughed softly.

''I wondered how long it was going to take you to get around to doing that. There are half a dozen people out there, so I have to go back out. But I'll be back at the rear door as soon as everyone else leaves.''

He bent, pulled down the top of her dress, and kissed the swell of her breasts.

''Little darling Thelma, you be back as soon as you can. I have a real problem I think you can help me relieve.''

She patted his crotch and felt the hardness. ''I'm sure that I can solve that one. Maybe solve it three or four times.'' She grinned, adjusted her dress, and went out the door to the living room, where they were straightening up before closing for the night.

O'Grady lay in the grass and weeds across the street in a vacant lot that faced Senator Douglas' headquarters. Beside him Lacey Eckstrom pushed up nearer to him.

"Looks like they're closing up shop," she said.

"Good, it's almost nine o'clock."

"So, who was that man we followed here? Could you see him when he went in the door?"

O'Grady shook his head. "Not enough. But as I remember, there's only one tall, thin man who works in that campaign headquarters. He's the senator's campaign manager, Randolph P. Alacron. I talked to him this afternoon. He asked me about the attack on Mr. Lincoln."

"But if he's been in cahoots with Barnaby and Kirk all along, he would have known about the attempt on Lincoln," Lacey said.

"Yes, but he would ask to throw off suspicion. And he might not have known who was captured and who got away. He and Kirk must have been working up some more dirty tricks for Mr. Lincoln. I'm almost sure that Senator Douglas doesn't know about this. If nothing happens tonight, I'll tell Douglas tomorrow and have him bring in Alacron for some tough questions."

"You think they might have plans for some deviltment tonight?"

"They can't do it any sooner. Evidently Alacron wants no debates. He must be afraid that the talks would give Lincoln a lot of good publicity and comments in the press."

"But kill Mr. Lincoln?"

"That would solve a lot of Alacron's problems."

Two men and a woman came out of the house and walked down the street away from the pair in the grass.

"How many left?" Lacey asked.

"Not sure. When the lights go out, we'll figure everyone not living there has left."

The lights went out downstairs five minutes later. The lone light upstairs had been blown out before.

"What are we waiting for now?" Lacey asked.

"To see if Mr. Alacron slips out for a midnight mission somewhere or other."

"I'm never going to see my bed again," Lacey whispered in a plaintive wail.

"Your turn for a nap," O'Grady said. "You go to sleep and I'll wake you if something happens. You have your gun in your reticule?"

"Of course."

"Good, you might need it. Now go to sleep."

"I don't get to sleep on your lap?"

O'Grady grinned in the dim moonlight. "Now that was nice."

"I'll get by without a lap," she said. Lacey lay her head on her folded arms and soon she dropped off to sleep.

O'Grady had to fight to stay awake. He could see the North Star, but he couldn't find the Big Dipper. Too early, maybe. He waited what he figured was an hour.

Lacey had mewed twice like a small kitty and turned over on her side. Canyon wondered if it was a wasted night. Probably nothing was going to happen. O'Grady decided he would hold out until two-thirty, then give it up.

A horseman rode by at a trot and it woke up Lacey. She leaned up on her elbows and stared at Canyon. "What time is it?" she asked.

"Don't know, and I can't strike a match to find out.

117

Early yet. If nothing happens by two-thirty, we'll head back to the hotel.''

"And sleep to noon."

"Absolutely."

"I think tomorrow I'll carry around a blanket with me. Then wherever I am, I can just lay down and have a good sleep."

"Good idea," O'Grady said, but Lacey didn't hear him. She had fallen asleep again.

What Canyon figured was an hour later, nothing had moved around the house. He sat up and turned his back to the house across the street and struck a match close to his body. He read his watch and blew out the match.

It was nearly two in the morning. He considered waking up Lacey, then hesitated. A soft sound came from the front porch of the Douglas house. Then a screen door screeched for a half-second. A shape came down the front steps and paused. The form looked lean and tall. It was the same man. Alacron.

O'Grady put his hand over Lacey's mouth, then shook her shoulder. Her eyes popped open, surprise in them, then she saw him and nodded.

"Looks like our tall thin friend is going for a walk. I think it's a good idea for us to follow him."

They kept well back but close enough not to lose him. Soon it was evident where he was going. He waited at the back of the Ottawa Hardware Store, and less than two minutes later Kirk came from the other way and unlocked the back door. Both men vanished inside.

"Now it's getting interesting," O'Grady whispered.

Five minutes later the two men came out. One lugged a tin pail or can or bucket of some kind, and the other carried what looked like some thin rope.

They moved out the alley the short way, away from O'Grady and Lacey.

The agents followed them closely. They went down two blocks away from the Douglas headquarters, and O'Grady grunted.

"Heading for Lincoln's house," he said softly.

"What are they carrying?"

"Don't know. We'll find out soon enough. If anything happens, we nail them before they get away. Shoot them if you need to. You can aim low if you don't want to kill them. In fact, it might be best. We need the kingpin."

By then they had come close to Lincoln's headquarters house. The two men paused across the street, then went down the street past it and came up behind the place. There was no other house directly behind it.

Kirk ran forward and seemed to examine the foundations of the house. They had been covered with shiplap all the way to the ground, with no foundations showing.

The small man ran back to Alacron, took the big can or bucket from him, and hurried back to the front corner of the house. He pushed the can against the house where a small indentation was left for a window. Then he seemed to push something into the can.

A moment later a match flared.

"It's a bomb," O'Grady growled. He drew his six-gun. "Get out your gun and go stop Alacron. Shoot him if you have to. I'm going to see if I can stop that bomb from going off!"

O'Grady raced forward toward the spot where he saw a bomb fuse sputtering fifty feet away.

14

O'Grady ran hard, pumping his arms, feet pounding the ground. Halfway to where the bomb's fuse sputtered, he bellowed at Kirk, "Noooooooooooo."

Kirk dropped the match he still held, and started to run away. O'Grady fired his six-gun. Kirk's arms flew up in the air, his feet stumbled, and he slammed backward onto the ground and never moved.

O'Grady raced on to the bomb, knelt in front of it, and looked at the burning fuse. It was two feet long, lots of time. He grabbed the fuse where it went through the side into the covered can.

He yanked on the fuse. It didn't budge. The damn thing was probably tied inside so it couldn't be pulled out. He grabbed the can and ran away from the Lincoln house. The bomb was heavier than he figured, maybe twenty pounds. He stumbled as he hit the street, but he didn't fall and surged on into a vacant area. He looked at the fuse as it burned closer to the powder in the big can. He ran on another ten feet, then he set the bomb on the ground, raced another fifty feet, and dived into the grass and weeds.

That whole area of Ottawa lit up with a brilliant flash as the fuse burned into the black powder. The explosion sounded like all the artillery shells O'Grady had ever heard going off at the same time. It sent a blast toward him that slammed him back to the ground from which he had lifted up an inch.

The booming, thunderous roar rattled doors and broke windows and turned the surrounding block into day for a fraction of a second.

When the blast passed, he sat up. A cloud of blue smoke shrouded the whole area for a moment before a gentle breeze began blowing it eastward.

O'Grady stood, remembered Lacey and the other bomber. He ran back the way he had come, surprised that his legs still worked. He saw Kirk's body where it had fallen. Another thirty yards on he saw shadows, and when he rushed up, a tall man standing next to the side of a house. As Canyon raced closer, he saw that the man was holding his shoulder, red seeping between his fingers.

Lacey stood six feet in front of the wounded man, the revolver held in both hands aimed at Randolph Alacron's heart.

O'Grady slowed down and walked the last few feet. He grinned at Lacey. "Looks like you caught a rat in our trap," he said.

Alacron sputtered in pain and indignation. "O'Grady, do something about this wild woman. I was simply out for a stroll before settling down to go to bed when this crazy woman screamed at me and demanded that I stop. I saw her gun, so I ran, assuming that she was a robber."

"Won't work, Alacron. Kirk is dead but he told me the whole thing before he cashed in," Canyon lied. "He said he figured you shouldn't get off free as a bird. You really must have been afraid of letting the debates go ahead."

"Oh, damn," Alacron said.

"My guess is that the senator doesn't know anything

121

about how you tried to help him by killing Abe Lincoln.''

"Of course he doesn't know. Damn you.''

Half a dozen people ran up, some of them in night-clothes. They asked what happened. O'Grady asked them the same question. One of Lincoln's bodyguards approached, a rifle in his hands. O'Grady went over and talked to him a moment, and the guard nodded and returned to the house.

By then two deputy sheriffs had arrived, and one of them went to fetch the doctor.

"Better get this one down to the jail where he can share a cell with his two partners in crime," O'Grady said.

Lacey lowered her six-gun and stood there as the deputy walked Alacron off to jail. Although her weapon was now pointed at the ground, she still held it with both hands. O'Grady led her off a ways and gently took the weapon from her clenched hands. The revolver had not been cocked.

"Oh, Lord, I shot that man," Lacey said, trembling.

"You certainly did. Otherwise we'd have a hard time proving that he was here and part of the conspiracy and the actual assault on Mr. Lincoln.''

"But . . . but . . . Then he stopped and I pointed my gun at him again, and you were right, he wasn't a paper target, he was a real, live human being. I couldn't have shot him again. I didn't even cock the weapon." She shivered. Then she grinned. "Glad it was dark so he couldn't see the hammer.''

She looked at O'Grady for a moment, then leaned toward him and collapsed against him. His arms came around her and he held her tightly.

"Easy there, United States Field Agent Eckstrom. Easy. You're just having a normal reaction to the sudden action. Happens to all of us, especially the first time we have to shoot somebody." He began to walk with her back to the hotel. "Did I tell you about the first time I shot a man?"

She looked straight ahead, her arms still around him. It made walking a little awkward, but neither of them complained.

"I had been an agent for about a month, and I came into a bank in a little town in Missouri and stumbled right into the middle of a bank robbery. There were three of them. . . ."

Lacey looked up and shook her head. "No, I don't want to hear about it. I just want to get back to the hotel. Please."

They walked the rest of the way in silence. Upstairs at her door she unlocked it and caught his hand and pulled him inside. He found the lamp and lit it, put on the glass chimney, and then turned up the wick to flood the room with pale-yellow light.

"Tonight, Canyon O'Grady, I don't want to have to turn out the light, and I don't want to have to stay alone." She looked up, a small frown on her pretty face. "Oh, I also don't want to make love. Can you stay here with me and hold me and be with me for a while? At least until I can get to sleep? I'm not sure I'll be able to sleep. Christ! I shot a man tonight. You told me it would be different. You just didn't tell me how different it would be." Tears slid down her cheeks.

He guided her to the bed and sat her down on it, then he knelt and took off her shoes.

"Dress?" he asked.

She shook her head. He pulled off his boots and fluffed up a pillow and she lay her head down on it. A moment later she sat up. She pushed the pillow away and leaned toward where he sat against the brass headboard. She caught his arms and brought them around her, then nestled down with her head on his chest.

"I think this might do it," she said, and closed her eyes.

He bent and kissed her cheek. Her eyelids fluttered but didn't come open.

"O'Grady. I hope this is tempting for you. I'd be a little disappointed if it wasn't. But I'm trusting you not to take advantage of my troubled state of mind."

"Miss Eckstrom, I'm tempted like all get-out. But I'm also smart enough to know when to show a little compassion. Your pure white body is as safe right now and for the rest of the night as if you were at home with six brothers guarding your bedroom door."

A soft smile creased her face, then she gave a big sigh and he could feel her relax.

"Good night, O'Grady," she said softly.

"Good night, Eckstrom," he said. A moment later she slept.

She woke up two hours later. He wasn't sure she knew he was there. She slid down on the bed and found her pillow and bunched it under her head. Then she reached for one of his hands and pressed it to her chest and held it tightly with both hers.

He slid down beside her and let her sleep. He fished his watch out and checked the time in the glow of the lamp. It was three-forty-five.

About five o'clock she woke, sat up, and looked at him. She pulled out the top comforter and slid under it, motioning for him to do the same. Then she pushed over next to him, pulled his arm around her, and nestled against his side. She went to sleep at once.

This time he edged toward sleep himself. As he balanced on that knife edge between wakefulness and sleep, he tried to remember if he had ever slept in a bed with a woman and not made love to her. He wasn't sure, but he didn't think he ever had. Then he slept.

It was nearly ten A.M. before he woke the next time. When he opened his eyes, Lacey sat on the bed beside him, chin in her hands, watching him.

"Good morning," she said.

"Have you ever said that to a man in your bed before?" O'Grady asked.

"No, silly, of course not." A small cloud settled over her features, turning them into a frown. "Did I . . . did I really shoot that man last night or was it all part of the dream?"

"I'm not sure what the dream was, but you put a bullet through Randolph Alacron's shoulder and captured him and held him until I got over there."

"And the bomb, that terrible explosion? It didn't hurt anyone?"

"Might have if a window broke at the wrong place. I couldn't stop it in time. That was an extremely powerful bomb they made."

"Mr. Lincoln is all right?"

"Yes, one of his bodyguards told me last night that he was safe but concerned."

"Oh, good." She looked out the window. Then in a very small voice she began, "Last night . . . I mean, did I . . . did we . . . ?" She turned and looked at him all little girl and vulnerable and trusting and wanting to believe.

He reached out and kissed her cheek. "Last night you were tired and you were emotionally spent and questioned a lot of things, and we sat on the bed, took off our shoes, and went to sleep. Once you woke up and crawled under the cover and pulled them over me. We slept, and that's all we did."

"Oh."

"Well, from your reaction, Miss Eckstrom, I'm

worried. I can't tell if you're relieved, or disappointed, or a little of both."

She grinned. "Damn you, O'Grady, you can read my mind. Yes, I'm relieved, because if we had made love and I didn't remember a thing about it, I would be furious. I guess . . . I guess I'm also disappointed because here I had you all to myself and I could have had you teach me how to make love, but instead I let you get away."

"Women always will be one great big contradiction to me. It's all right. I accept that as fact. Now, why don't you wash your face, let me go to my room and shave, and I'll buy you a working man's breakfast?"

"Done," she said, bouncing out of bed.

"Bouncing" was the right word, O'Grady decided as he watched her full breasts jiggling and moving. Oh, the wonders and glories of a good woman.

A half-hour later they sat in the dining room downstairs in the Plainsman Hotel and worked on that thresher's breakfast: four fried eggs and half a plate of country-fried potatoes, hotcakes with butter and hot syrup, bacon, sausage, apple sauce, toast with jam, and coffee.

After the meal they sat back and worked on a third cup of coffee.

"If that's what threshers eat, I think I'd like to sign up on the crew," Lacey said.

Sheriff Tillery came in the dining room, looked around, then walked up to the table where the two agents sat. " 'Morning. Figured I might find you here," he said. "Mind if I sit down?"

"Help yourself, Sheriff," O'Grady said. "How about some coffee?"

"Had too much already. I hear you did some good last night. Also hear you forgot to mention the fact that you left a dead body lying around."

"Oh, him. Yeah. He just didn't seem important at the time. More worried about the live one. You need a report?"

"Yes and more. Senator Douglas is screaming at me this morning. Says I don't have enough evidence against his man Alacron."

"We'll be down there in ten minutes and give you sworn statements, notarized, that will be enough not only to hold Alacron but to convict him. A little pressure on Barnaby and Pike should turn up more evidence. What we might do is offer them a lighter sentence if they testify against Randolph. You've still got both of them in jail, don't you?"

"Oh, yes indeed. No bail for either of them. Do need them affidavits, though. You might have a talk with the senator as well." He paused and twisted in his chair.

"Fact is, I'd appreciate it if all three of us could go see the senator right now," O'Grady said. "I'm sure he can fit us into his busy schedule."

Senator Douglas scowled as the three of them walked up the stairs to his private quarters.

"Sheriff, this better be good. I've got a certain amount of power in this state."

"Senator, this county elects me sheriff. You have no vote here. I think you should hear what these people have to say about your former campaign manager."

O'Grady looked at Lacey. "Senator, last night Agent Eckstrom and myself witnessed Randolph Alacron confer with the deceased Kirk Danzing after working hours in the back of the Ottawa Hardware Store. We followed Alacron to this headquarters and then about two A.M. followed him back to the store. He and Danzing came out with what later turned out to be a powerful bomb.

"They carried the bomb to Mr. Lincoln's headquarters, placed it below Mr. Lincoln's room, and lit the fuse. Mr. Alacron was captured as he tried to escape the site of the bombing and was shot in the shoulder and captured by Agent Eckstrom. There is no doubt he tried to kill Mr. Lincoln last night, and at least three other times within the past week."

Senator Douglas sat down in his chair. He shook his head and took a big breath that came back out as a sigh.

"You just never do know a man. I've worked with Randolph for almost fifteen years now in one way or another."

"He wanted nothing to interfere with your winning this senatorial election and then the presidency, Senator Douglas," Lacey said.

The senator stood and stared out the window. "What will be will be. I'll bow to your evidence, pay for a good lawyer to defend him in court, but assume that he's guilty and will be severely punished. In the meantime, I'll need a new campaign manager." The senator turned. "Thank you, miss and you gentlemen, for stopping by."

At the sheriff's office, the two agents wrote out their depositions and had them notarized. Then they walked out into the fall sunshine.

"One threat down. Now, what about that damn Nymon?" O'Grady asked.

"If we had a company of cavalry we could mount sweeps through the camping spots within ten miles of Ottawa," Lacey suggested.

"But we don't, so we can't."

"So, we watch and we wait," Lacey said.

"At least I know what Marcella looks like now."

Lacey bristled. "That is the understatement of the

century. You know *exactly* what she looks like with and without her clothes on."

"Easy, easy, nice lady. You be nice and I won't tell anyone that I slept with you last night."

"You did no . . ." Lacey's angry face turned into a grin. "You have the better of me on that one. So, what can we do? Walk the town?"

"Sounds good. If we split up, we can cover twice the space. You take the west side of Main Street and the businesses on that side, I'll take the other half."

"No fair, you get Delmonico's," Lacey said.

"We can meet there for dinner or supper, or whenever you're hungry."

"Supper, about five o'clock today."

"Done. Now get to work." O'Grady watched her walk away. It was pleasant work. She had changed clothes and now wore a light-green form-fitting dress that had a little bustle that now twitched delightfully as she walked across the street.

O'Grady continued down Main not exactly sure what he was watching for. The Nymon gang wouldn't come back into town until the day before the debate, or maybe a day sooner.

He went past a leather shop where a man was working on a saddle. The smell of new leather drew him to the door. Leather had a special fragrance about it that made O'Grady want to be a saddler. He looked inside, and for a moment he thought he was seeing things.

A pert, pretty redheaded woman sat on a stool, her skirt up over her knees. She wore a diamond necklace and diamonds on her ears and wrists. Marcella Quiney, the sexy redhead from Nymon's Raiders, smiled at him.

"Mr. O'Grady, just the man I've been looking for. If you have a few minutes, I'd like to talk to you." She smiled again, slid off the stool, and vanished through the long strips of rawhide that had been cut from a single piece of leather to create a movable curtain in front of the back room.

O'Grady hurried inside the leather shop and through the rawhide-strip curtain.

15

Canyon O'Grady saw no one besides the saddler as he walked into the leather shop and through the leather strips that formed a curtain over a door to the rear. As he parted the leather strings, he saw the girl waiting for him.

Marcella stood beside a small cot and a table piled high with just-tanned cowhides. For a moment she smiled, then the smile faded. "You ran away from me last time, O'Grady. I don't like that. Did you have a good reason?"

"As I remember, you were the one who ran away. I heard shooting, and when I came back, you were gone."

"Life can be hard sometimes." She smiled. "But I'm back. The saddle maker is a friend. We can use his place without being disturbed. Come."

"What happened to your blond hair?" Canyon asked.

She ignored the question and went through the door into a well-appointed apartment. It looked like the inside of a home with furniture, even a window with a view on the alley and the plains beyond.

The girl sat in a chair and waved him to another. "I thought you would be gone from this small place by now," she said.

"Fascinates me. I thought you were on your way to the railroad. You get sidetracked?"

"Matter of fact, I did. Ran out of money. A regular problem of mine."

"You could always cash in a diamond or two."

She touched the necklace and looked at the bracelets sparkling with stones. "Never! They're heirlooms, my dear mother owned them. It was all she left me."

"Just one of those small ones would take you to the best hotel in Chicago."

"I've been there. I'm thinking of riding down the Mississippi on one of them riverboats all the way to New Orleans. That's why I came back. I want you and me to go down there together."

She left the chair and came up to him; she kissed his lips, then pulled his face into her breasts. "Of course, all of me goes on the trip. You were good the other night. It could be that good, making love all the way down the old Mississippi."

He pulled his face away so he could breathe. "Honey, I've heard that story before." He stood. "What was it you said your name was, Mary Jane? Well, Mary Jane, a girl as pretty and sexy and as available as you are, just doesn't travel around the countryside alone."

She watched him, moved her shoulders so her breasts jiggled.

"Oh, yeah, I know I'm right about this. You got to be something you're not saying you are. I figure some big bruiser is going to come in here in a minute and push a forty-five in my stomach and demand all my cash for being indecent with his wife."

She took a step back. She pouted. "Oh, hell, you're right about part of it. Might as well tell you. I did have a man. Met him right after you took off that morning. We headed for Chicago, but the second night

132

on the stage he got mean and hurt me, and I told him to jump in the river and took the next stage back here.

"And the diamonds aren't real. Just fake. But I love to wear them 'cause the hicks out here don't know the difference. But I do need you; I want a handsome man like you who wouldn't hit me and hurt me, and who is so good in bed it just gives me gooseflesh all over my little old body even now just thinking on it."

She watched him and he let her see that he was almost buying it. He would, too, if he didn't know who she really was.

"Maybe you need to see the package again. Got all this wrapping on it. But that comes off." She caught his hand and pulled him toward another door. It led into a bedroom. There were no more doors. One small window was curtained. She closed the door and pushed a solid bolt firmly in place.

"There now, nobody's going to disturb us. We can just talk and kiss and . . . and anything you want to do. Right here, right now. And then I want to talk again about going to New Orleans. I hear it's the most romantic place in the whole world. Just puts that Paris, France, place to shame."

As she talked, she unbuttoned the front of her dress; then, in one swift move, she lifted the garment off over her head and stood there watching him, her bare, big breasts swinging and bouncing from pulling off the dress.

"Delicious," O'Grady said. "Downright delicious."

"Then don't be bashful. Have a few chaws on my titties. Lord knows that's all they been good for so far."

"Who was this other guy you went away with? What does he do? The one you dumped down the stage line?"

"Why you want to know?"

"Curious. We got to have something to talk about while I'm chawing off these big tits of yours."

"Yeah! His name was Sam Seward and he was a . . . I shouldn't tell you." She looked down at him as he sucked in one breast and chewed on it. "Okay, okay. He liked to rob banks. He never hurt nobody, and I told him he better not. I didn't mind him robbing banks. People who have so much money they need to put it in banks can afford to lose some. But I wouldn't let him slap me around no more. I told him that, and he hit me again. So, when I went to the woman's convenience at the stage station, I just stayed there and let the stage drive off with Sam screaming and yelling that they left somebody behind."

The half-naked redhead gave a sigh. "Now, that's more than enough talk." She pushed O'Grady back on the bed and unbuttoned his fly and went right to work.

"This is what I call the best part of a man, his old dong, his prick. Look, it's getting hard already!" She jumped off the bed and kicked out of her petticoats and loose silk drawers and stood in front of him naked. Slowly she did a little dance, then got on her hands and knees on the bed and bent over his crotch. She pulled down his pants and drawers and moaned.

"Oh, glory, I'm gonna give you a honeysucker. You ever had a real good old-fashioned honeysucker? I'll show you how. You don't have to even wiggle, just lay here and let me do it all."

She pulled his erection from his underwear and yanked the offending garment down farther, then lowered her mouth to his thick pole and kissed it top to roots.

"Oh, yes," O'Grady said. "I'll tell you when you can stop."

"Joke's on you. I'm not gonna stop, not till you buck and mouth-fuck me and you come all over my face." She dropped on him then, sucking half of his rod into her mouth and bobbing up and down.

It had been a while since a woman had serviced him this way. The more O'Grady thought about it, the more excited he became. But that wouldn't find out what he needed to know from this girl.

He pushed her away and sat up. "You're enjoying that too much. I'm still mad that you ran off with another man. We had a good thing going."

She frowned and sat there watching him. "Said I was sorry. What more can I do? Offered you a honeysucker. Damn, most men piss and squeal if I offer them that."

"I don't like the way you took off with that guy. Hell, who can you trust these days?"

"Trust me, big man. Trust me to get you to New Orleans. We can have ourselves one big wonderful sexy time floating down the old Mississippi."

"I want to know the man's name. Who you run off with that way and leave me?"

"Told you once. Sam Seward . . . If he knew I told, he'd kill me."

"So maybe you're not a whole hell of a lot better-off now. Don't like my women fucking anybody else."

"Who says I'm your woman?"

"You come to me, you want me, you're my woman long as I say. Otherwise get your dress on." O'Grady started to stand up.

She pushed him down gently. "Okay, okay, don't get so mad. Probably never see him again. His name's really Sam Seward like I said. He's on a few wanted posters. You can check."

"Don't think you went on the stage at all. I think

135

you slipped out of town and camped along some creek. Your hair smells like new grass and sweet red clover.''

She looked up sharply. ''Oh, damn. Not many men got that good a nose. Yeah, we camped awhile. We went about five miles west of town toward La Salle on the river. Nice little spot. Just Sam and me. He said he wanted to get my ass in the grass and he sure as hell did. But I run out on him. Grabbed the saddle horse and hauled in here to town.''

''So he'll be looking for you. When he finds you, he'll try to blow my head off.''

''No! Oh, no. He said good riddance as I rode off, and he went on to La Salle.''

''Did, huh?''

''Well, sure. Now come on, poke me with that thing. I'm getting an awful itch there inside.'' She spread out on the bed, lifted her knees and pushed her legs wide apart, inviting him.

He went between her thighs and stroked her nether lips. She moaned. ''Oh, yes, darling. Right now!''

''That camp, why don't you and me go out there? I've never had a woman like you naked in the grass. Be fun. Where is it? We need a buggy or do you fork a horse?''

''Darling, let's talk later. I need you deep inside me right now! Please, sweet darling.''

The more she begged, the more her southern accent came back.

He stroked her again, worked his lance across her lips, and touched it inside then came away.

''Sure you're telling me true about this man? I heard there was two of them, both bank robbers.''

She scowled at him, stuck out her tongue. ''Damn you! I need you in my pussy now! Come on. Oh, hell, yes, there were two of them, and they robbed two

136

banks, and then they got mean and I ran away and they're probably looking for me right now."

"Sure, and they'd kill me if I fuck you. You trying to get me killed here, Mary Jane?"

"No, no, they won't do that. Just wanted to find out if you was still in town. There now, I said it. So do me good, little darling with the big stick."

"How far out on the river?"

"About halfway to La Salle, five miles maybe."

"On this side of the river?"

"No, the other side." She stopped. "Why you so interested? You some kind of marshal or something?"

"No, not a marshal. I just wondered. You want to show me the place?"

"Oh, no, I couldn't do that. Then they'd get real mad. I'm going to Chicago and then to New Orleans. Want you to come with me. I'm more than willing. I even got considerable money."

In a sudden move he lanced inside her, then pulled out and teased it around her slot.

"Don't do that! Don't torture me this way. I need it. I want it deep inside me right now."

"Two of them out at the camp? Just two?"

"Yes, damn you!" She tried to be angry but her body wanted him more than her anger could overpower.

"They expect you to come back and tell them about me, right?"

"Yes, yes. Now do me, twice at least!"

He went into her hard, jolting her upward on the bed, slamming again and again with no thought of her until he exploded. Then he came out and watched her writhing and moaning on the bed. At last her hand went down, found her clit, and rubbed it until she climaxed three times.

She sat up and stared at him. "Bastard."

"You got what you wanted."

"Part of it." She found her dress and lifted it up, then suddenly she pulled a derringer from the skirt pocket and swung it toward him, but he was ready for any surprise. He hit her arm, forcing the weapon down just as she fired.

The round going off in the small room sounded like a cannon. O'Grady had forced the gun down as it discharged and the bullet had slashed through an inch thickness of her thigh and buried itself in the mattress.

She screeched in pain and anger as he took the two-shot weapon away from her.

"Well, Marcella, you shot yourself. Damn untidy of you to do that."

She looked up at him, well aware of his use of her real name.

"Yes, Marcella Quiney, twenty-two years old, former whore from New Orleans, now the woman of one Flint Nymon. Oh, you told the truth about Flint being a bank robber. But not that part about him not hurting anyone. He's a vicious killer, as you well know. Afraid you're not going to be able to report to him about my status. I just hope you told the truth about where his camp is. If not I'll be back to talk to you again, in your jail cell."

"Jail? What the hell, I ain't done nothing."

"You've harbored a wanted fugitive, you've ridden with the outlaws after they robbed the La Salle bank. I saw you the next day. I was the one who got ahead of you and winged Dade Matzner. Remember the old west motto: you ride with outlaws, you hang with outlaws. You'll get to talk to Dade about it in jail."

He found a piece of cloth and tied it around her leg to stop the bleeding, then threw her the dress.

"Put on some clothes, unless you want to walk to the jail bare-assed like you are."

She pouted as she dressed, but he wouldn't let her

touch him. She was a whole body loaded and ready to go off at any second.

They went out the back door to the alley. O'Grady didn't see the saddle maker anywhere. He might not even know who the girl was. Time enough for that later.

At the jail, Sheriff Tillery tipped his hat in surprise. "This the one who rides with Nymon? Damn but she's a looker. And a fancy lady, you say."

"True. Lock her up where Dade Matzner can't get to her. Then the doc better take a look at her leg. Poor thing shot herself with a fancy little derringer. Adding the piece to my collection."

"Charges?" Sheriff Tillery asked.

"Assault with intent to kill against me. Harboring known outlaws wanted by the sheriff's department. That should hold her for a few days. Don't let her out for any reason until we get this mess cleaned up."

He saw the girl put in a jail cell. She had pulled her dress down to expose one breast and had almost managed to get the deputy's gun who was locking her in. After that everyone was more careful.

O'Grady signed two papers as a complaining witness, then went out and walked the street for a half-hour before he found Lacey. She had just come out of a woman's dress shop and looked a little embarrassed.

"Yes, I was taking some time out to look at the dresses. I enjoyed it. No, I haven't seen anything of the Nymon gang. It's only a little after midday. You interested in a cup of coffee and some dinner?"

"You'll never keep your girlish figure eating this way."

"Will too. I run it off. We can argue over some food. I'm thinking about a big roast-beef sandwich. Suppose we could get one at Delmonico's."

They got two of them.

16

When the sandwiches were almost gone, O'Grady told Lacey about his confrontation with Marcella Quiney.

"You saw her right here in town?"

"Yes, and now she's in jail. She tried to shoot me with her derringer but hit her own leg instead."

Lacey frowned and leaned closer to him so she could whisper. "Was she naked at the time of the shooting?"

"Yes," he said, and grinned.

She looked pained for a minute, then shook her head. "Men! I guess you'll never change. At least I don't want the job to try to civilize you. So where is the rest of the gang?"

"I found out where they might be, if she isn't lying. I'm going out there this afternoon with a pistol and rifle and see what I can find out."

"I'm going with you. It's my job."

"It's not your job to get shot at."

Lacey lifted her chin. "It isn't your job to get shot at either. That's why I'm going with you."

"Lacey, don't push me on this. If you try to go with me, I'll never tell you a single thing more about this case. I'll freeze you out and keep you alive. I . . . Dammit, I don't want to see you get hurt. These men are killers, both of them."

"I'm getting paid to take that risk, just like you

are." She settled down. "I'm still mad, just mad as . . . as hell. But I don't want you to be angry at me. Maybe this time I should stay here. When are you leaving?"

"Soon as I can get my clothes changed and rent a horse from the livery."

"The hostler will probably make you buy it before he lets you take a horse this time."

"Probably."

She stood. "Well, you see what you can find out. I'll check the security around the site for the debate. They're building a big outdoor platform for the speakers and putting up some bleachers, I understand. People will be coming into town from all around."

He watched her, wondering at her sudden change of mind. Maybe she was worried about being shot at, after all. Whatever it was, he was pleased.

He stood. "I can walk you back to the hotel. I'm going that way myself."

A half-hour later, O'Grady rode out of town west along the river road. Marcella said the gang was camped out about five miles out and on the south side of the river. He'd have to find a place to cross over, a ford where he wouldn't get too wet.

He decided Nymon would be camped in a heavy growth of trees and probably wouldn't be watching the trail. No telling how long Marcella would be in town. He'd go into the woods about four miles out and work forward slowly to be sure he didn't overrun them or get spotted riding up.

He figured the two men would be eating, drinking, or sleeping—enjoying the good life after their two bank holdups. The woman was gone, so they would be drinking.

O'Grady rode steadily but in no rush. He couldn't move up on them close until after dark anyway, or at least dusk. Once he turned and looked behind him but saw no one. It wasn't an often-used trail. Most of the trade went to the east.

About three miles from town he stopped at a small stream running into the larger Illinois River. He stepped down and let his mount have a drink and chomp on some new grass. A horse and rider burst out of some light brush near the river, and before he could get to his six-gun, he saw who it was.

Lacey Eckstrom brought her bay to a stop beside him and grinned. "You didn't think you were going to get away from me with a quick argument like that, did you?"

"I was a bit surprised."

"Now you know why. I had to get changed and get a horse, too. How much farther is it to the camp?"

"You're not going."

"Who made you boss on this job? Field agents cooperate; we work as equals, not as big brave hero man and dumpy little woman who washes out his socks."

O'Grady laughed. At first he'd been mad when he saw her; now he was pleased she was along. "I should spank you and send you home."

He saw anger flare on her face.

"But don't get your britches on fire. I'm not going to. Damn I guess I'm getting used to having you around. I hate to admit it, but you have helped us get as far as we are on this case. So, hell, stay if you want to."

"The great man actually gave me his permission. I'm overwhelmed. How much farther to Nymon's camp?"

He walked over and looked at her gear. She had a canteen, a blanket roll, a small sack of what could be food, and a carbine in the boot.

"How far? Another two miles, unless little Marcella

was just making up a story. Figure we'll get there about dusk, move up and challenge them. They'll put up a fight and we might get one of them.''

''Why don't we attack them earlier? If we wait till dusk, they might get away in the dark.''

''Yeah, but if we try to go in earlier, they might spot us and kill us both before we know where they are. We'll take what we can get now and hope for more later.''

She watched him a minute, then bobbed her head. ''All right, I understand. Another two miles?''

''Probably. We have time to move slow and be sure what's ahead of us.''

They rode.

Fifteen minutes later they angled into the trees along the river. He still hadn't found a good place to ford. Now they watched and found what looked like a long sandbar that stretched out into the Illinois at a wider spot.

''We need to be on the other side, and this looks like a good place to go across,'' O'Grady said. ''Can you swim?''

''Like a fish.''

''Ever swim a horse across a river it couldn't walk across?''

''No.''

''Let's hope you won't need to.'' O'Grady studied the water for a minute, then started forward. ''Follow right behind me, but if I drop off into deep water, wait until I get to the other side.''

They moved ahead slowly across the sandbar, then into the silt-filled river as the sandbar faded. The water came up to their feet, then halfway up on their legs as the horses maintained a grip on the bottom.

They kept at that depth for another twenty feet and

then the bottom sloped up and they were out and on the other side. They were wet up to their knees.

"A cheap crossing," O'Grady said. "I've made lots worse. Once I had to get off and swim and hold on to the reins of my horse Tarmac."

They sat on their mounts in a patch of sunshine and let the water seep out of their clothes. Then they dismounted and pulled off their boots to empty the river out of them.

Ten minutes later they were riding again. They stayed in the brush and trees along the river now as they worked downstream. O'Grady checked his pocket watch. When he snapped open the front cover, he saw that it was just a little after three. He found a spot of sun ahead and stopped and stepped down from his horse.

"We're early. We better wait here for an hour or two. Not polite to come to a party this early."

"Especially when the host doesn't know we're going to be dropping in," Lacey said.

"Also, I figure they won't have anything to do but drink whiskey. I'm counting on them being drunk by the time we get there."

"Trouble is the report said Nymon can shoot just as straight drunk or sober," Lacey said.

"Thanks for the reminder."

They sat on the sunny spot of grass and watched the river.

"Why did you become an agent?" Canyon asked.

"Same reason you probably did. It sounded exciting. I'd get to travel, I get some good training, and the pay was good. Besides, I wanted to be the first woman agent. It took me almost two years to get approved."

"Reason I joined was I couldn't hold down a steady job anywhere else," O'Grady said.

She punched him in the shoulder with her small fist.

"Where are you from?" he asked.

"Washington, D.C. My daddy was a senator from Virginia for twelve years, and then he stayed in town. A lot of senators do that. He's still working in government."

"Brothers, sisters?"

"Two brothers, older; two sisters, younger."

"So you're in the middle. That must be why you're so hard to get along with."

She narrowed her eyes and watched him. "Sometimes I can't tell when you're teasing and when you're not. That's one of your big problems, O'Grady, that I'll put in my report. You see my real job in the agency is to team with another agent, go through a case, and then make a detailed and exhaustive report on his ability, personality, competency, how he works with people, the whole professional rundown. So far I've had two agents fired and got raises for three others."

O'Grady looked at her sternly for a moment, then he chuckled. "Almost got me that time. But when you're lying or teasing, there's a little crinkle at the corner of your eyes you can't control. It always pops out, like now."

"Damn. I'm trying to control it. I'll put your chuckle into my report as well. It just might save your job."

Now he looked at what she was wearing. She had on a dull-green blouse that blended in nicely with the woods. It buttoned down the front and high to her throat and covered her arms to her wrists. The blouse was straining over her breasts, but he decided the damn buttons would hold. She wore a split skirt that let her ride astride and covered up everything well except that little round bottom, which still twitched as she walked.

She lifted to her knees and was close beside him. "Canyon, there's something else I wondered about,

145

strictly in the area of gathering information." She reached out and kissed his lips. Her eyes closed and she held it a moment. Then she pulled back. Only their lips had touched.

"Well?" he asked softly.

"Not sure," she said.

He reached out and pulled her to him until her breasts crushed against his chest, then his open mouth covered hers and his tongue washed at her lips until they opened and for a moment they clung to each other. Then he eased away and let her go and leaned back.

"Oh, my, yes! I think I can give that kiss a favorable report. There will need to be considerable more, er, research in that area." She grinned. "What that means is, damn you're a good kisser!"

He grinned and stood and lifted her to her feet. "Thanks for your approval. I need a raise."

She laughed.

"We better be moving. Another mile, maybe. But it will be slow. You have that six-gun loaded?"

"Yes, it's a thirty-eight-caliber six-shot. I have five rounds in it and twenty more in my pocket. Yes, I can reload fast enough. This is a special solid-cartridge model made in France. It works."

"The rifle loaded?"

"One round. Single shot. I have lots more. It's a fifty-two-caliber Sharps-Hankins carbine, experimental, but I love it. Yes, I'm qualified on it."

He nodded and they moved again, working along the trees, skirting open spots. The river made a large bend south and they followed, then he stopped and motioned her up beside him. "Smell anything?" he asked.

"Smoke. We're downwind of a camp fire."

"Very good. You may pass yet. Yes, smoke. If it's

Nymon, he would have a small fire now, just to keep it going. Maybe. Slow and easy."

They dismounted and walked, leading their horses. They had finished rounding the bend in the river and gone no more than a quarter-mile when they saw where smoke drifted out of a heavy brush area three hundred yards ahead. It was nearing six in the afternoon and they had another hour before dusk.

They tied their horses' muzzles shut with bandannas so they wouldn't horse-talk with the two mounts that must be downstream a ways.

Then they took their rifles and moved up slowly through the woods and brush toward the smoke. The light was failing inside the woods. They worked up cautiously, not making a sound.

Slowly O'Grady lifted up to look over a fallen cottonwood log. Thirty yards ahead he saw the opening toward the river. The other side was heavy with brush. Two men lounged around a small fire and passed a bottle back and forth.

The voice came floating to Canyon faintly.

"Crunch, you no good bastard. You have never done an honest day's work in your life."

Crunch tipped the bottle, lowered it, and wiped his mouth. "Yeah, Flint, never one damn day. I'd rather be like you." They both howled in laughter and Flint Nymon tipped the bottle.

O'Grady dropped back down and fell partly on Lacey, who had wormed her way up beside him. His hand rested on one of her breasts and he eased away from her. "Sorry."

Her glance met his and she smiled. "You don't have to be too broken up about it. What did you see out there?"

He told her.

"You believe what they taught us about never firing first?" she asked.

"Never have fired first yet. Of course, that means if they reach for a gun or other furtive move, we can fire. Can you use that carbine?"

"Yes."

"Good. I'm moving up another ten, fifteen, twenty yards. You cover me. If they hear me and pull a gun, shoot one of them. Shoot the smaller of the two. Got it?"

"Yes . . . yes. I'll cover you." She pushed the carbine over the old cottonwood log and nodded.

He worked around the log and crawled forward through the brush and leaves.

She lost track of him for a moment, then watched how slowly, how quietly he worked toward the camp fire. She moved once to keep him out of her line of fire, then settled into the former spot. He was fifteen yards from the two outlaws when she saw him level his six-gun over a small log.

"Put up your hands Nymon. You're under arrest," O'Grady bellowed.

Two six-guns roared, but before Lacey could get off a shot, both outlaws dived out of sight.

17

Canyon saw Nymon surge to the left to try to get out of the line of fire. O'Grady fired, automatically tracking the man, but he figured his round missed. Then there were no targets. Both men were suddenly out of sight. He hadn't heard the rifle fire. Damn.

O'Grady lifted up a moment, then jerked back down. A six-gun blasted a round into the top quarter-inch of the log protecting him. Somebody out there was good with iron.

O'Grady rolled down six feet to get a better angle at the tree Nymon must be using for his protection. Something else moved. It had to be Crunch. The big outlaw, flat on his belly, shifted position, and one leg slanted out from the small log he was cowering behind.

The U.S. agent took careful aim with his six-gun and fired. Crunch bellowed in a roar of pain, sat up a minute, and then lay back down. Another roll and a front dive and roll and O'Grady came up behind another tree that gave him a perfect view of the back of the little camp. He had moved far enough so he could see plainly where Crunch huddled.

Nymon wasn't there. The darkness closed in more. O'Grady searched all of the small camp but couldn't find Nymon.

"Give it up, Crunch. I've got you from behind. Not

a chance in hell you can shoot your way out. Your buddy ran off and left you. I got six men out there just waiting to nail you.''

Crunch sat up and waved his gun. "You ain't got me, you bastard. I'm gonna grind you up into dust and mud and brain juice!" He stood and started moving toward O'Grady's tree. The agent stepped out and fired a shot past the big man, then aimed at his heart.

Before Canyon could fire, a snarling sound came from the brush behind them, and a .45 round jolted into his left arm, spinning him around, smashing him down to the weeds and the grass, and sending his six-gun bouncing away out of reach.

Crunch laughed. "Told you I'd get you. Gonna tear your arms off, then I'm gonna kick you in the balls and watch you scream. Next I'm gonna swing you around like a rag doll and slam your head against a tree until it splits open and your brains drain out.''

O'Grady struggled to stand up. His left arm wouldn't work. He backed up, scrambled upright, but the big man was four feet from him, his ham hands reaching, fingers already in claws waiting to tear him into pieces.

O'Grady dived for his six-gun, but Crunch kicked it out of reach. He thought of going for the hideout derringer, but the little gun wouldn't stop Crunch. Anyway, there wasn't time. Fractions of a second now. Where the hell was Nymon? Why hadn't he shot again?

Then Crunch was almost on him, the big man's hand touching O'Grady's shoulder. The darkness was closing in as well.

The shot came like a cannon's blast in the silent woods. Crunch stopped where he stood, his hand swung down as if it was suddenly too heavy to hold up. His eyes went wide and then his mouth opened and he gasped for breath.

Then O'Grady saw the blood. It gushed out of his

mouth in a red splattering torrent. Crunch's knees buckled and he knelt down, then twisted and fell on his back, his big hands falling limply at his sides.

Canyon lunged away from the body, half-dived, and then rolled to where his six-gun lay on the ground. He grabbed it and darted six feet behind a big tree that would shield him from the direction Nymon had taken.

Only then did he realize who had saved his life. Only then did he realize that Lacey had shot Crunch with her carbine. He looked at Crunch and then to where Nymon had fired from. He bent over and ran back to the log where he had left Lacey.

She sat there, the Sharps-Hankins resting on the log again, the breech closed and a spent round on the ground below. Two unused cartridges lay on top of the log. Her legs were crossed, both hands on the log, her eyes staring straight ahead at where Crunch must have stood when she fired. She didn't turn or move as he sat down beside her. He lay his pistol on the log and looked at her. His left arm hung useless at his side.

He put his good right arm around her and felt the tension, the rigidity of her body. He smoothed her hair back, kissed her cheek, and began talking softly.

"It's all right, Lacey. You did what you had to do. None of us likes to kill a man. It hurts. It's wrong. But sometimes that's the only way. If you hadn't shot Crunch, I'd be dead and probably you too."

She relaxed a little and leaned against him. Her head turned. "He was going to hurt you. I had to shoot him."

"Yes, Lacey, you did exactly right. He was a killer, a bank robber. You're a lawman, you had to shoot him."

"But he was a human being. I never planned on having to kill anyone. I don't know . . ."

"Hey, you'll be fine. Nymon is still out there. He

may try to kill us before the night is over." It was fully dark then and he had to peer closer to see her. "Best thing we can do is go back to our horses and get you a blanket. But first, I need you to help me. Can you tie up my arm? Nymon hit me with a shot."

Her eyes widened and then she frowned. "Yes, your arm. Let me help." She took the handkerchief he gave her and found where the bullet had hit him high in the upper arm. She tied the handkerchief around the wound.

"I'll fix it better when we find our horses. I have some cloth we can use."

"Thanks for the bandage. It feels better already. The bullet must have gone right through. Now we better get away from here. In the morning we'll figure out what to do."

It took him a few more minutes to convince her, then they stood and walked back to their horses. They untied their muzzles and he watered both and let them munch on fresh grass. He took down the blanket and lay it out for her.

In her sack she found some squares of cloth. They were picnic napkins. They folded one and used it as a compress and used another one to tie the cloth over the wound. When she finished, the bleeding had stopped and the arm was feeling a little better.

He knew not to offer her anything to eat. He did bring some water from his canteen, and she drank, then lay down on the blanket. A moment later she whimpered and called to him.

He sat down next to her and she held out her arms. He held her, whispering to her how it was all right, how these things happened.

The tears came then, and they washed through her like a flood, leaving her sobbing and gasping for breath. Then she lay back down on the blanket and held out her arms again, and he lay beside her, whispering and talking softly, his right arm around her. Gradually her sobbing and gasping stopped and she drifted off to sleep.

Twice that night she woke up screaming. He was there and held her close, and she whimpered a little and then went back to sleep.

He drifted off to sleep sometime during the night and was awake with the first tinges of dawn. For a minute he didn't think he could move his left arm. Then he worked at it and found it to be stiff but not as sore or as useless as before. He could bend his elbow and use it a little. It would be fine for the rest of the day.

He found ground coffee and metal cups in her sack of supplies and made a fire and boiled some coffee for them. She woke up suddenly and he saw her eyes; they went wide in terror before she realized where she was and who he was.

"Oh, God, I killed a man yesterday," she said.

He looked at her as she sat up. Her brown hair was mussed, her green blouse had two buttons on the top open, showing a V of white throat. Her divided skirt looked unrumpled and smooth as the day it was made.

"Yes, you killed a man, but you also saved my life. I thank you for that. I'm relieved that Crunch is dead; both of us could be lying back there with our heads smashed in."

She watched him a moment and then nodded. "Yes, I understand that. I just have to come to terms with it in my own mind." She sighed. "Is that coffee ready?"

"Thanks for bringing it. I don't plan ahead that far."

They sat around the small fire. When the coffee was done, he put out the fire to reduce the chance of Nymon finding them. He watched her as they drank the hot brew.

"Today we have a tough job. We have to go back to the camp and find where they kept the horses and then track Nymon out of there and try to capture him."

"Maybe I should ride back to town," Lacey said.

"No. You're a field agent. I need you here. Know anything about tracking a horse?"

"No."

"Then you'll learn. I can't do this by myself."

She looked at him curiously, then shrugged and helped him clean up and repack her sack of goods and tie it on her bay.

They rode back to the campsite and went around the corpse, searching the brush until they found the other horse. When they found it, O'Grady got off his and began walking a big arc around the site.

Five minutes later he called softly. "I found his trail. Over here. He left last night, and was moving fast. No idea where he's headed."

She rode and led his horse and he followed the trail. It curved out of the brush to the south of the river, then turned back toward the east and Ottawa.

In the open country away from the river, the trail was easy to follow. The horse had been galloping along here. He showed her how to tell the difference the way the hoof threw dirt behind the print, and how the hoof slanted in a little more when it hit the dirt instead of coming down more at the vertical.

At a small stream the hard-riding Nymon had paused to give his mount a drink and a short rest. There were several horse droppings there and O'Grady took a stick and broke one apart. He stared at it a minute, then came over to where Lacey still sat her horse.

"If I was an expert, I could tell you exactly how long ago that horse stood here. As it is, I'd only be guessing. My thought is that Nymon must have ridden most of the night to be sure he got away from us.

Nymon is not a leader who takes care of his men. He never even tried to save Crunch last night. He thinks only about his own safety and well-being.''

They rode again. They had just come over a small rise and could see Ottawa three or four miles away to the east and north when a swishing sound slapped the air between them where they rode eight feet apart.

"Down," O'Grady thundered. He slid off his horse, reached up and grabbed Lacey. He lifted her out of the saddle and they both fell to the ground. He was half covering her with his body.

Then the crack of a high-powered rifle came to them from far across the small valley.

They lay there a moment and he moved so he wouldn't crush her.

"What was that swooshing sound?" she asked.

"That was a rifle bullet passing within three or four feet of each of us. At least now we know how Nymon is going to try to kill the debaters."

"With a powerful rifle from a long ways off?" Lacey asked.

"Yes. He must be doing a little target practice."

They lay there for another minute, then he moved off her completely. "Don't sit up. He might not be through."

"How far away is he?"

"Half a mile, maybe farther."

"He couldn't even see us from there," she said.

"Not unless he mounted a telescope on top of his rifle and zeroed it in for long distances. I've seen a few. They're heavy but deadly accurate, I've heard."

Five minutes later they sat up.

"He must be gone," O'Grady said. He helped Lacey up, then caught their horses. They were grazing only a dozen yards away.

They mounted and Canyon looked at Lacey. "We're

155

not going to find him. As soon as he hits a road with any traffic, we'll lose his prints. We might as well head back to town and see what we can do about picking out some sighting lines of fire—pretending that we were going to be shooting the debaters.''

Later that day when they got back to Ottawa, they went to the doctor's office and he patched up O'Grady's arm.

"No big problem here," the medic said. "Round went right through; it cut a few small muscles but they'll repair. Gonna be sore for a month or so. Take care not to strain it and see me in three days for a fresh dressing.''

Next they went to Sheriff Tillery and told him about the body out in the woods, five miles out. He sent a deputy and a spare horse out to bring in the corpse and at the same time marked down as solved the bank robberies in La Salle and Cottonwood Bar.

For the next few days, Lacey and O'Grady rode around town checking out spots that could be used by a sniper. They climbed ladders and stood on store roofs; they even went into the Baptist church bell tower. The sexton assured them that the tower's trap-door was locked at all times and no one was permitted up there.

Twice they stood on the hardware store's roof and checked the angles.

"This has got to be one of the best spots in town," O'Grady said. "The false front would give Nymon a spot to shoot from so nobody can see him. Both the speaker's stands can be seen plainly from here and we're only a little over a hundred yards from the plat-form.''

The hardware store was closed because Kirk Danzing was dead. Before they left the premises, O'Grady got a hammer and tore down the first ten feet of the ladder up the back of the building so no one could climb up without a lot of trouble.

They checked out the small bluff just in back of Main Street. It looked right down the street at the speaker's platform. From two hundred yards the shooter would have an open aim. This was getting frightening.

"There must be ten or twelve good places to shoot from around here," Lacey said. "We've got to call off the debate."

They went to the principals, but both absolutely refused.

"This is a political debate," Douglas said. "I'm not about to let some gun-toting outlaw cow me into not appearing."

"He could shoot you dead."

"Thy will, not mine, O Lord," Douglas said.

Mr. Lincoln put it about the same way.

"Nothing we can do but put deputies in all the most obvious spots from where Nymon could shoot the debaters, and then hope we catch him in time," O'Grady at last decided.

Sheriff Tillery checked each of the ten locations with them the day before the debate and hired extra deputies to control the crowd expected and to man the potential assassination positions.

The night before the debate, Lacey and O'Grady had an early dinner, then went to their respective rooms for a long sleep. They had agreed they would meet at five-thirty the next morning and patrol the worst sniper positions until after the debate was over.

"All we can do now is hope and pray," O'Grady said.

18

Both agents were up and walking the area by daylight. They met at the platform and each stared out at the surrounding buildings and the bluff and wondered where Nymon would be hidden. He might be there already, laughing at them. Or he might come in some disguise and slip into position halfway through the debate when everyone was tired of watching for him.

"Damn him," O'Grady exploded. "He could be anywhere. We've got to get the debate called off or somebody is going to get killed."

"We've tried."

"We'll try again. First let's check out our ten most possible spots." He threw a thick rope over the lowest rung on the ladder up the back of the hardware store and went up to check. There was no one hiding on the roof. He let himself down from the roof by the rope and hammered out the rest of the rungs of the ladder on his way down.

They checked the bluff and the eight other spots, including two residences and two more store roofs.

The debate was set to start at ten in the morning. It was then just after seven A.M.

They went to each of the candidates and carefully explained that they had seen Nymon and had killed another of his men, but that he still was out there and he had a big gun like the one people shot buffalo with. It was deadly up to half a mile away.

Both candidates listened to the arguments, then shook their heads and said the debate must go on.

"Let's go to the sheriff. He has the power to cancel a public gathering if he thinks there's danger. The gunman could kill a few citizens before he hit the senator or Abe."

Sheriff Tillery laughed at the idea. "I have to get elected again in two years. Half the people in the county would hate me if I canceled the talks. Hell, it's a big holiday for the merchants here, too. Besides, I just can't justify the public-safety idea. What we have to do is nail this guy before he can shoot."

"How?" Lacey asked.

"I've put on twenty-five extra deputies. We need some of them for the crowd, but I figure ten of them can watch for the killer."

"They can cover the ten most likely sniper locations, stay there all the time," O'Grady said. "Yes, that will help. The three of us can circulate, check the locations, look for others. The way that platform was set up, half the town seems to offer Nymon a vantage point from which to shoot."

The three walked around town posting the deputies at the hot-spot locations. There were hundreds of people in town already, and more were streaming in in wagons, surreys, and buckboards.

"So, that much is done," Sheriff Tillery said after they had posted the deputies, each with his silver star showing. "You sure about this Nymon character? Will he really try to come in here and shoot the debaters?"

"You've read his wanted, seen my official papers on him. I know he'll try. He's probably in town right now waiting. All we have to do is find him."

"You know the town will be filled," the sheriff said.

159

"I hear folks talk about relatives coming in from as far away as fifty miles. We could have five thousand people here before that talk starts. Got people and rigs parked all over the place now, and more keep coming."

"Merchants must love it."

"Indeed they do."

"Any more suggestions for us, Sheriff Tillery? Where would you set up if you wanted to kill these two men?"

"Where?" They were standing below the platform and already people were putting up benches in the street. Main Street for two blocks had been shut off from wagons and horses. The sheriff looked around. "One would be Ma Linnerly's boardinghouse. Right there in the jog in the street. The city fathers didn't have the heart to make her tear it down. She got a lawyer who said her house was in that spot before the city got fancy and measured out the streets. Look at those two upstairs windows."

"Aren't the curtains moving on that one side?" Lacey asked.

"Probably. It's going to be a warm day, lots of folks open the windows about this time of day," the sheriff said.

"I'll go see the lady, Sheriff, talk to her. Ask about any new boarders who came in during the last four days, any with rifles or long boxes."

"Sheriff, any more locations we could check?" Lacey asked.

"Matter of fact, I did some looking late last night. Here's a list. We covered some of them already. Take a look."

An hour later, Canyon and Lacey had checked out the last of the possible positions. Nobody looked suspicious. The town was filling up. It was a struggle just to walk across Main Street now.

They paused on the far side.

"O'Grady, this is an impossible task," Lacey said.

"That's why they gave it to us. All we have to do is stop the impossible. You keep making the rounds. I want to check that boardinghouse. Can't think of a better spot for Nymon to be hiding these last few days."

She nodded. "Hey, be careful."

O'Grady grinned and watched her. "You be careful yourself. We only have one woman agent. Think of the trouble I'd be in if you wound up getting killed. It would probably ruin my career."

She stuck her tongue out at him and walked down the street.

He knocked on the boardinghouse door and soon a sprightly little woman less than five feet tall opened it. "Yes sir?"

"Ma'am, I was wondering if you have a room available. Bet you're filled up with all the folks in town."

"Was. A gun salesman just left. You looking for a room?"

"Gun salesman?"

"Yes, handguns, revolvers mostly."

"Oh. Yes, I need a room for a few days."

"Two dollars a day board and room. Three meals you want them. Got the upstairs south room. Nice view. Fact is, you could watch the debates from up there if you want."

"Could I take a look at it?"

"Right up this way."

The hallway was papered, the staircase varnished to a gleam, and the stairs had a home-braided rag-rug runner. The room was nice, better than his hotel room, and the view was fine. He looked at the platform. Already there were half a dozen dignitaries on the risers. There was a stir in the crowd as the two candidates walked up the steps at the back of the platform. Sunshine slanted in the window.

"The room on the other side, is it taken? That sun hit this side hard, could get a little warm."

"Rented. Man came several days ago. Had a hurt on his arm, said he snagged it on a tree limb. Said he'd be leaving this afternoon."

"Is he there now? Maybe I could look at the room and take it after he leaves."

"It's my house, I'll ask him." She went into the hall and knocked on the door. O'Grady followed her. There was no answer at first. She knocked again, then called. "Mr. Jones, Mr. Jones, I need to talk to you."

"Later. I'm busy right now. Come back this afternoon."

"No, Mr. Jones. This is important. Come to the door please."

"Go away, old woman. I rented the room. Now go back downstairs."

O'Grady made a twisting motion with his hand as if turning a key. She saw him, nodded, and started to push a key in the lock. The door jolted open three inches. O'Grady was not where the man could see him.

"Need to show this room to a prospective renter. He wants it for a week. Now just step aside and let me show it to him," Ma Linnerly said.

"No. I rented the room. I paid you in advance. He can see it when I'm gone this afternoon." The man slammed the door closed and they heard the key twist in the lock.

"Mr. Jones! You open up this door or I'll get my rifle and shoot it full of holes until I hit you. You understand?"

162

There was no reaction.

O'Grady ran back to the other window and looked out. The speakers were in their chairs behind the two small podiums. A man in a frock coat was checking his watch. The debate was about to start.

O'Grady hurried back to the other door and pulled the woman away from it. He whispered to her. "I think there's a man in there who will try to kill the speakers. I'm going to have to kick down the door and stop him. I'm a United States government agent. I'll pay for the damage."

Her eyes widened and she stepped back. "Go ahead. I really don't even own a rifle."

He drew his six-gun, made sure that all six chambers were loaded, and looked at the door. He heard a cheer outside. Now was the time!

He ran four steps at the door, jumped, and planted his right boot against the panel just above the door handle and its flimsy lock. His nearly two hundred pounds of weight battered the door, smashed the lock, and slammed it inward, where it swung on its hinges against the wall.

Inside, O'Grady saw a man sitting in a chair with a long-barreled rifle that he had aimed out the window. The rifle rested on a second chair with a sack of flour to hold up the barrel.

O'Grady saw all this in a flash.

The next instant the man whirled and fired a six-gun. The round ripped into O'Grady's thigh, slamming him backward in the hallway and out of the line of fire.

He heard something in the room and the slap of a rifle round coming in the window. The bullet hit the chair holding the five-pound sack of flour, jolted it to the left, and knocked the rifle off the sack.

The man inside cursed. He shot a glance at the door,

saw nothing, and furiously tried to get the weapon back into his preset firing position. He used his six-gun to snap a second shot out the door into the hall and then settled the rifle back in position.

A second rifle round slammed into the room through the window, but it missed the chair. O'Grady crawled on his stomach up to the edge of the door. He lifted his six-gun and saw the man sighting down the rifle barrel, his finger reaching for the trigger.

O'Grady fired. The round hit Flint Nymon in the shoulder. He jolted to one side, turned, and fired twice at the doorway with his pistol, but his aim was too high.

"Give it up, Nymon, or you're dead," O'Grady shouted. The gunman started to lower his sights and O'Grady fired again. The round bored through Nymon's nose, going upward, and shattered inside his skull, chopping up a dozen vital brain centers.

The lifeless body of Flint Nymon slammed against the far wall and slowly slid down to the floor.

O'Grady knew there was no need to check on Nymon. He groaned at the pain in his leg and his left arm. He turned over and looked at the small woman who owned the boardinghouse.

She was scurrying forward with a pot of water and a cloth and some bandages. "Goodness, that must hurt fierce. My late husband used to get shot now and then. He was the former sheriff here, you know. I know all about bullet wounds."

She cut his pants leg both ways with a pair of scissors, examined the wound, and nodded. "Yep, slug went right on through. Not too much damage. I figure if I bind it up now, there won't be any more blood on the floor for me to clean up. That front room, though, I bet it's a mess. Know the sheriff'll want to be here."

Somebody knocked on the door downstairs. Ma

Linnerly got up and hurried down the steps. Lacey Eckstrom came in holding her revolver with both hands, ready to shoot.

"Land sakes, it's all over, girl," Ma Linnerly said. "They are both upstairs."

Lacey ran up the stairs two steps at a time and looked at O'Grady. She kissed his forehead and moved over to the right-hand room. She turned, wide-eyed, her palm covering her mouth. "Nymon?" she asked.

"What's left of him. That had to be you outside with your carbine. You messed him up good and proper. We would have lost at least one of the debaters without those two or three shots of yours."

"Glad to be of help. I saw the curtain moving, so I used the field glasses and spotted the gun barrel. Then I took up my Sharps and tried some target practice. I kept thinking there was a target there in the middle of the window and shot at that."

"Good thinking."

By then Ma Linnerly was up the stairs, and she finished binding O'Grady's thigh.

"Why don't I go find the sheriff?" Lacey said. "Then we can get this finished up. I want to listen to the rest of the debate."

Mrs. Linnerly frowned. "Oh, pshaw. I figured maybe you'd help me clean up that room. I know I can rent it tonight if I get it fixed up in time."

An hour later the body had been removed and Lacey and Mrs. Linnerly had the room cleaned up and presentable again.

"Now, O'Grady, let's get out there and listen to the last part of the debate. Don't you know those two men are probably making history? We can tell our grandchildren about it."

19

Lacey Eckstrom and Canyon O'Grady stood on the fringes of the big crowd and listened to part of the debate, then Canyon nudged her and caught her hand and they walked away.

"We have someone to meet at the Willoughby Inn. There can't be more than one or two people there who did not come up to watch the debate."

"Our foreign friends?"

"Could be. If the payoff was to be today as well, the conspirator won't have any idea when the deed is to be done, so maybe we can slip up on him without any problem."

They walked the three blocks out to the edge of town. The inn was still a handsome building, but a bit dated now. The manager hurried up as they came inside the front door.

"Ah, Mr. O'Grady, you're back. I haven't seen any more of those friends of yours. The two English ladies are still here, though. They told me they probably would be leaving tomorrow."

"Mr. Gunderslaugh, I'm glad to hear it. Are they in their rooms, do you know?"

"I'm afraid they're at the debate, as is everyone else."

"And no other foreigners?"

"No, I'm afraid not. The inn is full for the debate, but we'll be mostly empty tomorrow."

"Mr. Gunderslaugh, as an officer of the government, I'm asking you to show me the English ladies' rooms. It's within my powers."

The innkeeper hesitated, then nodded. "As long as you're working for the president. I voted for Mr. Buchanan, I did."

They went upstairs to Room 12 and the owner opened the room.

"I do hope you won't disturb anything. I'll have someone call if they come back, but I don't think they will."

O'Grady looked for a case that could contain money, a lot of money, $25,000 worth. He searched the closet, under the bed, in their empty suitcases, and in the small dresser.

Lacey was investigating the clothes. She looked up, surprised. "Now here is something interesting," she said, pointing to a dresser drawer. "This drawer is full of men's clothes. And there are pants and a man's suit in the closet."

O'Grady checked, smiled grimly, and put everything back the way it had been.

"Thanks, Mr. Gunderslaugh, don't say anything about this. Your nation thanks you for your cooperation."

They went downstairs to have a piece of cherry pie and cup of coffee in the small dining room as they waited. The English women said they would be back for tea right after the debate was over. It was expected to last about two hours.

Lacey couldn't help but fidget as she waited for the inn owner's wife to finish serving them the pie and mugs of steaming coffee. When the woman walked away, Lacey almost burst.

"So, the two English women are the foreign contact with the killers? One of the women is pretending to be a man so we wouldn't suspect them."

"That's the way I read it. Could be wrong, but a closer look and talking to them should prove interesting."

The pie was gone and they were on the second cup of coffee when the two English "ladies" came in the front door.

Mr. Gunderslaugh met them and asked them about the debate.

"A bit too much for us, dearie," the younger-looking woman said. "We had to nip off a bit early before it was over."

"Yes, we need to pack and all," the older one said.

O'Grady was up and walking toward the front desk. He looked behind him at the wrong moment and ran full force into the older woman. The figure bounced back, then tumbled to the floor. The person did a neat roll and was back on her feet in an instant. It would have worked perfectly if the wig had stayed in place, but the blond wig had jolted free and lay on the floor, revealing a dark-brown hair cut short, a man's haircut.

O'Grady lifted his six-gun smoothly. "Easy there, my good fellow," he said. "Too bad about the wig. You did very well for so long. You're both under arrest by the United States government for conspiracy to commit murder, the assassinations of Senator Douglas and Abraham Lincoln."

Lacey stepped up with her six-gun trained on the woman. O'Grady searched the man in the dress and found a small hideout derringer. Lacey did the work on the real woman and found another derringer in her purse.

"Now, upstairs, let's have a look at your room. I'm

sure we can find lots of interesting documents and the sum of twenty-five thousand dollars in cash.''

It took another two hours to find the written orders of the pair who were working for a British shipping firm. O'Grady and Lacey confiscated the $25,000 as evidence and turned the pair over to the sheriff for safekeeping until the Justice Department gave him instructions what to do with them.

People had started flooding out of the little town as soon as the debate was over. Nobody knew who had won. Some said Douglas did, but some said Abe Lincoln made him look like he was too soft on the slavery issue.

It took O'Grady another hour to find exactly what he wanted, then he picked up Lacey in a smart little black buggy with a white horse pulling it. He handed her in and showed her a picnic basket on the floor and two blankets to lay on the ground.

''We're off on a picnic, a nice calm little picnic by the river where nobody will bother us or disturb us.''

''Sounds interesting,'' Lacey said. ''Did you bring fried chicken?''

''Wait and see what I've brought for you.''

She picked out the place: a small grove of trees next to the Illinois River, a half-mile from the river road and about two miles east. A carpet of grass and wild flowers covered the ground.

The picnic was delicious: cold fried chicken, potato salad, a small crock of baked beans still warm, dill pickles, fresh-baked rolls and butter, and a pot full of brewed coffee Canyon heated up over a small fire. For dessert they had big slices of watermelon.

They lay on the blanket watching the water.

''How is the arm and the leg?'' Lacey asked.

''Now that you mention it my arm is itching-hurting,

so I know it's healing, but my leg is still throbbing."
He lay on his back staring up at the sky through the
trees.

She sat up and leaned over him. "Canyon, about
that girl."

"Marcella Quiney."

"Yes, that girl, that whore. Is she prettier than I
am?"

"No."

"Good."

"Forget about that girl. I was trying to find out some
vital information, and I did and it helped solve the
case."

"Would you treat me the same if there were some
vital facts you needed from me?"

"No."

"Why not?"

"I wouldn't trick you, I'd just ask you."

"I wouldn't tell you. That girl didn't."

"Forget that girl."

"I can't. You made love to her. You haven't made
love to me. I'm jealous of her."

He sat up. "She was a whore."

"She was a woman. I'm a woman."

"And a fascinating and marvelous woman."

"So?"

He leaned in and kissed her. She put her arms
around him and kissed him back, holding him tight,
pushing her breasts against his chest. He eased away
from her.

"So?" she asked.

"You're a lady."

"I'm a lady who wants you to make love to her."

"Right here?"

"Right here, right now, or I'll scream."

"I hate it when women scream."

He pushed her gently back to the grass and lay beside her.

"Yes, in the grass, outdoors," she said, and reached up and kissed him, holding his lips, not letting them go.

"Lacey . . ." he began.

"Shut up, O'Grady."

She unbuttoned her blouse and his hands explored her wonders. Later she pulled up her skirt and kicked off some thin, silk underthings. Neither of them undressed completely.

They made love gently, tenderly, as if it were the first time for both of them. Then they lay in each other's arms watching the sky and some birds and clouds sailing over high and unthreatening.

"Now, will you forget the other girl?"

"She's forgotten." Lacey reached up and kissed his nose. "I have much more wonderful things to remember."

They ate the rest of the fried chicken and had another slice of watermelon and then made love again, fast and wild and furious. Both were panting and wide-eyed when they collapsed together.

When they got their breath back, Lacey sat up and stared at him. "A girl could get to like doing this."

"Don't let that idea get around."

They both laughed and began picking up the picnic things and shrugging their clothes back into place.

"What happens next in this fieldwork?" she asked.

"We see what local law needs from us for any local cases. Mostly we leave depositions to be read in court, which is just as good as our being there. You know that, since you read for the law.

"This time I'd say we don't have much else to do. You can send a telegram to your friend Jamiston Priestly in Justice that the Nymon gang has been eliminated. Then we will wire our regular contact at the War Department telling him that this mission is finished and we're standing by here awaiting orders.''

"We'll have a few days?'' she asked, smiling.

"Maybe. Sometimes I get back a return wire with a new assignment. Sometimes they say come back to Washington, D.C., for a briefing."

"But tonight we'll be here, and we can . . . I mean, I'll be pleased if you'd spend the night in my room." She laughed. "Did I really say that? What a wanton I'm becoming. You seem to bring that out in me.''

"It's part of the satisfaction and the letdown when a mission is over. You know we probably won't work together again.''

"That's probably true," Lacey said. "I'll always remember this time with you because it was my very first field assignment.''

"A couple of other firsts, too.''

They drove back as it grew dark, and turned in the buggy and stopped by at the telegraph office to send the wires, one to Justice, and one to the War Department.

Then they hurried back to the hotel and into her room. She closed the door, threw the bolt, and put a chair under the handle as he had taught her. When she turned around, she was unbuttoning her blouse.

"Canyon O'Grady, I want to see you naked," she said.

He laughed softly and matched her button for button. It was going to be a wonderful night. Tomorrow a little business, then maybe a day or two before they got new orders.

"Hurry up, O'Grady, I'm getting ahead of you," Lacey said, and they both laughed, their eyes sparkling.

KEEP A LOOKOUT!

The following is the opening section from the next novel in the action-packed new Signet Western series
CANYON O'GRADY

CANYON O'GRADY #6

COMSTOCK CRAZY

June 1860, Virginia City, Utah Territory.
A town born out of "blue mud" and the lure
of fast wealth that now offered
only the promise of hard work
and sudden death.

Sweat beaded the medium-sized man's forehead and his eyes shot a quick glance at the door. It was too far away, and he knew he couldn't try, not and hold his head up again in this town.

Adolph Gathers swallowed, his prominent Adam's apple bobbing. Someone at a table close by laughed a skittish, nervous, glad-I'm-not-you kind of sound.

"Look, Loonin, I didn't . . ."

"That's *Mister* Loonin to you, Gathers. Say it."

"Mr. Loonin, I did not mean to offend you. I had no idea you were standing behind me and . . ."

The man called Loonin was well over six feet tall and heavily built, with shoulders stretching the blue checkered shirt he wore. Now his fist snaked out and slammed into Gathers' cheek, jolting him along the bar as he scrambled away trying to maintain his balance.

Loonin went after Gathers like a bare-knuckled boxer, smashing his fists into the man as he hung on the bar, until the last one, a solid right fist to the point of Gathers' jaw, sent him spinning to the floor. He hit a spittoon and it tipped over on his chest; the sour, fetid, brown juices splashing over him and soaking into his gray suit.

Gathers shook his head. For a few seconds he didn't seem to know where he was, then he pushed the spittoon away and started to stand up.

Loonin kicked him in the stomach when he was on his hands and knees, flipping him on his back. The big man laughed and looked down at Gathers.

"You learn to keep your goddamn mouth shut, Gathers, or next time I'll knock all your teeth down your throat." Loonin pulled his right foot back to kick the downed man again. When he started it toward Gathers, someone behind Loonin slammed the big man's foot to the inside and it hit his own left leg. Loonin went down in a tangle of arms and legs, bellowing in pain.

Gathers scrambled up and ran out the front door.

Loonin came to his feet bellowing in rage. "Who's the bastard who hit me?" he roared. "I want to see the son-of-a-bitch before I tear his head off."

A tall man near the bar took one more drink from a mug of beer and put it back on the varnished surface. With deliberate and calculated slowness he turned and stared at Loonin.

"I must be the son-of-a-bitch you're looking for. I never liked to see a big lummox taking advantage of a smaller man." The speaker was four inches over six feet, heavily muscled at 220 pounds and his hair was flame-red. He had crackling blue eyes set in a roguish face.

Loonin roared and hurtled the ten feet across the room at his new target. But the redhead wasn't there when Loonin arrived. He met only a sharp, stinging left jab to his nose and then, as he slammed past and hit the bar, a heavy fist powered down into the unprotected nape of Loonin's neck. His head snapped back and he almost passed out.

Loonin clutched at the bar much as Gathers had done before. The redhead stood four feet away watching him, his big hands at his sides where a fine leather holster was tied low on his thigh with a piece of rawhide.

"Stand still, you bastard!" Loonin brayed as he pushed himself erect. His fists came up in the classic pose as he moved forward. The redhead peppered his face with three hard jabs, bringing a spurt of blood from Loonin's nose before Loonin could even swing.

Again when Loonin lunged forward to hit the redhead, his opponent stepped away and this time tripped Loonin, sprawling him across a poker table while the four players hastily dove away for safety.

This time, Loonin came up with a chair in his hands and swung it as he advanced on his tormentor.

The redhead darted back, then forward as the chair passed him, caught the chair leg at the end of the swing and jerked it forward. Loonin saw his mistake too late. He had hung on to the chair and already was moving toward the redhead. Three more hard blows thundered into Loonin. The final one was a smashing right to the side of his head that traveled no more than a foot.

Loonin's eyes closed, his knees buckled and he fell backwards to the floor, unconscious.

For a moment the saloon was quiet, then someone laughed.

"By damn, never seen Loonin bested before by anybody," a voice said.

"I want to buy that man a drink!" another voice said.

The redhead stood, arms at his sides, watching Loonin as he shook his head trying to regain consciousness. He sat up and looked around, then found the man who had hit him. Slowly Loonin stood. He never took his cold stare off the redhead.

"Who the hell are you?" Loonin asked.

"Who the hell is asking?"

"My name is Rush Loonin. Always like to know the name of the gent I'm about to kill."

All talk in the saloon died. Men who had been standing behind the two now separated so there was an open space behind each one in case a bullet missed its target.

They stood facing each other fifteen feet apart, their hands hanging loosely at their sides.

"The name is O'Grady. Did it ever occur to you that the dead one might be the likes of you?"

"No!"

Loonin began his draw first. . . .